A WALTZ

CARAF Books

•

Caribbean and African Literature
Translated from French

Renée Larrier and Mildred Mortimer, *Editors*

A WALTZ

LYNDA CHOUITEN

TRANSLATED BY SKYLER ARTES

Afterword by Mildred Mortimer

UNIVERSITY OF VIRGINIA PRESS
CHARLOTTESVILLE AND LONDON

The University of Virginia Press is situated on the traditional lands of the Monacan Nation, and the Commonwealth of Virginia was and is home to many other Indigenous people. We pay our respect to all of them, past and present. We also honor the enslaved African and African American people who built the University of Virginia, and we recognize their descendants. We commit to fostering voices from these communities through our publications and to deepening our collective understanding of their histories and contributions.

Originally published in French as *Une valse* by Casbah-Éditions, Alger
© 2019 by Casbah-Éditions, Alger

University of Virginia Press
This translation and edition © 2025 by the Rector and Visitors of the University of Virginia
All rights reserved
Printed in the United States of America on acid-free paper

First published 2025

9 8 7 6 5 4 3 2 1

Library of Congress Cataloging-in-Publication Data
Names: Chouiten, Lynda, author. | Artes, Skyler, translator.
Title: A waltz / Lynda Chouiten ; translated by Skyler Artes.
Other titles: Valse. English
Description: Charlottesville : University of Virginia Press, 2025. | Series: CARAF books: Caribbean and African literature translated from French | "Originally published in French as Une valse by Casbah-Éditions, Alger, © 2019." | Includes bibliographical references.
Identifiers: LCCN 2024026133 (print) | LCCN 2024026134 (ebook) | ISBN 9780813952567 (hardcover ; acid-free paper) | ISBN 9780813952574 (paperback ; acid-free paper) | ISBN 9780813952581 (ebook)
Subjects: LCCGFT: Novels.
Classification: LCC PQ3989.3.C457 V3513 (print) | LCC PQ3989.3.C457 (ebook) | DDC 843.92—dc23/eng/20230612
LC record available at https://lccn.loc.gov/2024026133
LC ebook record available at https://lccn.loc.gov/2024026134

Cover art: Mask and hands, iStock.com/VPanteon, all other images Envato
Cover design: Elke Barter

CONTENTS

A WALTZ

Certainly solitude is dangerous for active minds. We require around us men who can think and talk. When we are alone for a long time, we people space with phantoms.

—Guy de Maupassant, *Le Horla*

In the middle of winter, I found there was, within me, an invincible summer.

—Albert Camus, *Summer*

At the Edge of My Madness

At the edge of my madness, a fairy is born.
She trades my heavy body
For a set of velvet wings
Draws another me I do not seem to know
She sings softly and sometimes smiles
At the kindly shadows
Awaiting her, welcoming
And they, captivated, hail her *houri*'s beauty.
At the edge of my madness, the fairy worries still
And soon panics
When the boors whistle
When the shrews whisper or their children laugh.
At the edge of my madness, the fairy ceases to be fairy
Her body swells,
She chokes and struggles for breath,
Sags beneath her weight, then dies, smothered.
At the edge of my madness, she is born again as bacchante,
Who, in fire, idolizes
Mirthful loves
That shift into deafening orgies!
At the edge of my madness, dream creatures,
Demons, satyrs,
Hate each other, then draw near
And, all together, toll the bell of a sanity now come to its end.

—Lynda Chouiten, August 28, 2018

EL MOUDJA

I

"Sublime. I will be sublime in this dress."

Chahira cast a satisfied glance at the flounces she had patiently and meticulously just finished embellishing with fine white lace. Proud of the beautiful garment she had created, she lovingly held it up to her body and hummed, eyes closed:

Layali el uns fi Vienna
Nasimha min hawa el ganna
Nagham fi el gaww louhranna
Semeeha el tir, baka ou ghanna*

Mohand, delighted, opened his eyes wide and smiled sweetly. Others gave a sigh of admiration.

"Thank you. You're so sweet," she whispered. "I looked everywhere for this lace. In the largest haberdashers in the capital and in Tizi."

Yes. Everywhere. Luckily, there was Ammi Amar the Aesthete and his lovely shop, Dragonfly. He had genially handed her the precious guipure lace while she was admiring the small crocheted tablecloths displayed on the shop's walls, the embroidered and smartly folded napkins, and the tiny ballerinas in tulle, just as fine and ethereal as the fragile insect that loaned its name to this magical place.

Ammi Amar had asked whether she also wanted tulle, and she had nearly said yes. But the warm amber fragrance that filled Dragonfly suddenly became a blend of odors—specifically,

* O nights spent in Vienna, in pleasant company!
The cradling breeze flows from paradise
It is a melody with a song that fills the air
The bird, hearing it, cried and then began to sing.

fish and sweat. But she had taken a bath this morning! She had panicked. She had thanked him and quickly left . . .

She would soon get to work on the sleeves. She wanted them to be poufy, like the ones she had seen in period-piece films, the ones worn by actresses plump and willowy alike. Decidedly, yes, this dress would be beautiful. And she, who was tall, though no longer as thin as she had been just a few years ago—she, whose delicately traced features had started to show signs of exhaustion but whose complexion had kept much of the freshness of her twenties, could appear nothing but elegant. And she would outshine all those bland Europeans—she, "the little Algerian," who up until now had known only the towns of Tizi N'Tlelli* and El Moudja,† the tiny village where she had spent almost her whole life.

She had been hunched over her work for more than two hours; her break had been well earned. Also earned was the pleasure of surrendering to the temptation of her little mirror, which, from the corner of the table where she always left it, persistently invited her to look at herself. She would not put it down for at least ten minutes. Just as she had done on the previous night and the day before, just as she did every day, she would gauge the beauty of her face. She would admire the oval shape, the rounded chin at once decided and pouty, the symmetry, the fine sculpture. All of it, she knew before looking, would satisfy her. Then she would linger over other details with more concern. She would study the contour of her eyes, searching for the slightest line. She would not find any—or nearly any—but her eyes would seem slightly lackluster, and she would notice the appearance of two small brown spots. Barely noticeable, true, but she could see them only too well. Her skin's tightness had also started showing signs of fatigue, and a few new strands of white adorned her beautiful auburn hair. A sudden panic seized her, along with an urge to cry. She had always been secretly proud of her beautiful face—was it, too, going to betray her? Leave her by the wayside?

---

* *Tizi N'Tlelli* (Kabyle): "Liberty Peak."
† *El Moudja* (Arabic): "The Wave."

She held the little mirror about twenty centimeters away, smiled, and looked at herself again as she shook out her hair. Agh! How stupid she was to be worrying herself like this! She had never been prettier, and decidedly, no—no one who saw her would think she was just six months shy of her forties. Yes, forty. Mohand acted surprised each time she brought up her age. Unbelievable that he showed so much astonishment, that he never remembered the number—she "talked" about it all the time.

II

And Mohand. How long had he been there? Five years? Six? The first time he appeared, she thought he would be her only ghost and would eliminate all the others. That she would learn how to tame him and he would be both the friend and the lover she had never had. What did it matter if she was the only one who could see him? She knew he was real. The others knew this full well, too, even though they wouldn't say so. For were these things to say?

She really liked Mohand. He was a bit like her: a nice young man whose hopes and ambitions had met with disappointment. Why hadn't he gone to school? Was he not smart enough? What troubles held him back? Brutal parents who repeatedly told him he was good for nothing, that he was a failure? She gave a small laugh: those were words she had heard only too often. Had a tactless elementary school teacher crushed his heightened sensitivity? For Mohand was sensitive, and she loved him for that too. But he was also a pessimist who lacked self-confidence. She sometimes tried, during bouts of mental logorrhea, to convince him that he was anything but a failure—that he should reach for his dreams.

"Release the artist inside! This guitar you barely let sing— why don't you let the whole world hear it? Why don't you believe this could happen? What if those who love your music sang your praises? What if you became famous? When that day comes, I hope you remember this voice, this female ghost that gently whispered in your ear that you could become someone. I ask for nothing more."

But he obstinately refused to believe this and became annoyed each time she tried to "talk" with him. He answered with growls of impatience and disagreeable words—*shit* or some other curse word lobbed in anger.

Mohand spoke very little; he was usually content with exclamations or vague rumblings. But when he did speak, his words were always in Kabyle. This was not surprising, because he was a Kabyle, a real one. In his accent, his tastes, and his way of being. His tastes and his way of being? What exactly does that mean: the Kabyle way of being? Mohand was a reserved boy who appreciated simplicity and good sense. Were those Kabyle values? Well, the girls she had known at Lalla Zineb were not at all like that. The high school girls in the city competed with one another, wearing trendy—though sometimes eccentric—outfits, and annoyed the village girls, who suspected them of showing off with their French, its accent more impeccable than its grammar. As for the village girls, they loved to tell salacious stories peppered with an audacious vocabulary and cut through with sonorous laughter. Some recited bawdy old poems the older women had taught them, and she, though shocked, could not help but find them clever. Later, she would discover that El Moudja's women sometimes recited the same type of poems in Arabic. And yet, whether in Kabylia or elsewhere, this country's women were supposed to be examples of modesty, right?

All the other ghosts also spoke in Kabyle. How was this possible? Her neighbors in El Moudja were not Kabyle. In this village, which had nothing poetic about it apart from its name and the sea that inspired it, people only trusted Arabic. Whoever spoke in French was impious and a traitor to the country's values; whoever spoke Kabyle was suspected of being in the former colonist's pocket. Yet her own ancestors spoke this language that the Moudjaouis found harsh, like the mountains in which it was born.

They—her ancestors—had carried their accent with them when, a century before, one of their own had accidentally murdered a rich and influential man, which forced them to flee the ire of the victim's family. Why had they chosen this forgotten place, far, even today, from the joys of the modern world? Was it because the sea assured them that they were far from their mountains and therefore safe from all reprisals? Was it because of this land's bounty, so different from that difficult land they had left? Or was it that the Moudjaouis from back then were much more amicable and welcoming than today's? Maybe, since the mountain people they had once been rushed to marry the daughters of this coastal region, which gradually adopted them. Little by little, they forgot their elders' language, so much so that Chahira's father knew barely a few words from this language which now only drew suspicion.

So then, why did the "others" speak Kabyle? The "others" . . . well, they included Nacer, the educated and well-raised boy who was also a bit fussy, a bit of a spoiled brat. His fastidious manners got him into a few predicaments. Judging by how angry he got each time the idea of homosexuality crossed her mind because of a television program, something she had read, or her very own thoughts, which sometimes liked to venture through redoubtable abysses, she sensed that people must often have assumed he was gay—that he had been subjected to unflattering sobriquets in that vein and that he must have suffered on account of them. She, on the other hand, did not believe for one second that he was gay. On the contrary, he was an exquisite lover. Ah, the wealth of delicacy she discovered that night—that lone and singular night! The flowers he had covered her in, and those ethereal caresses! One would think he had grown up elsewhere, in a world other than that of the boors—or, at least, the hard-hearted—who surrounded her. Nacer gay? Never! But, of course, in this accursed country, a delicate man was surely a fag.

Nacer was a nervous one, just like Mohand—and just like him, a man of principles. These two were the only ghosts who withstood the male desires she unwillingly fueled. Their bodies on fire, they did not dare approach her; castigation was their only recourse to soothe their panicked flesh. But Nacer was better educated and more sophisticated. These two nervous ones—the artist and the intellectual—were her favorites, or at least the ones she knew best. Among all those whose strange company she endured, they were the only ones she knew by name. The "others" included innumerable men, young and less young, whom she could not name and females she imagined as fat and common and who, unlike the "males," produced no sounds apart from laughter. The foolish laughter of *merqouchettes:* brainless women who think they are clever.*

---

* Unlike with other Arabic words, the author does not offer a translation of this term in the original text. *Merqoucha* is a derogatory term for a common, though not necessarily unattractive, and undistinguished woman.—*Trans.*

III

Hell is definitely other people, a certain philosopher once said. Chahira smiled unconsciously while telling herself this for the nth time. A little seamstress from El Moudja citing Sartre! But it was not Sartre she cited the other day when that short, chubby gentleman—chubby like the one standing next to her now in her makeshift workshop—had brought her a pair of pants to take up . . . Oh, yes, it was Plato. It was he—the short man with the ruddy complexion—who had referenced him first. He had been overly insistent that she do a good job for him, and as she grew irritated by this, he felt the need to justify himself. He had said ironically that he would have been more at ease living in Plato's Republic where everyone—seamstresses included, of course—had their place.

"And where, I imagine, you would have been philosopher-king."

She had been all smiles when she said this, but the barb of her sarcasm was all too evident. The flabbergasted look on his face! That made the young woman smile now. Upon hearing this, did he tell himself that this seamstress from El Moudja was decidedly not in her place? By the way, where exactly was a seamstress's place? How conceited! She had made a point of flaunting what she knew. Of course she was upset that he had taken her for a poor, uneducated artisan. Yes, hell was definitely others: they size you up, judge you, find you fat or ugly or clumsy or stupid or ignorant.

But she could not take any credit for knowing Plato. She had just remembered her classes at the end of high school, that was all. Mr. Ouahab Rouha was one of those rare teachers who, too steeped in learning and reflection to deliver a coherent and well-structured lesson, communicated their passion more than they actually taught. Back then, his students had nicknamed him the Philosopher. They listened to him construct the most puzzling series of questions about justice, reason, morality, and art—according to Plato, according to Aristotle, according to Kant, according to Nietzsche, according to Sartre, and according to so many others—and drank in his words, fascinated, though a bit uneasy at seeing shaken what they held as certainties. But it seemed they always foundered on the baccalaureate exam. They thought too much on their own and dissertated conclusively, when all they needed to do was just pretend—to regurgitate memorized definitions.

And what grade would she have gotten on the exam? Would the Philosopher have also trapped her in an overly exhausting spiral of questions for the exam graders? She was quite sure she would get it, this famed diploma, the most important of them all. Except she never would. The "others" did not want her to. Hell was also this: seeing herself forbidden to reach the end of her studies, just a few months before the end of her secondary education, when she was so bright.

She suddenly touched her left breast. That heat! The gentleman who had just dropped off a jacket—she was to sew the buttons back on—took a small step back. His back was turned, of course, but she thought she saw a roguish smile cross his face. He must have been delighted, the bastard! In his filthy little mind he imagined touching her, and now the sensation at her chest would linger for at least an hour. Until then, what other parts of her body would be "violated," as they had been the day before, as they were all the time? If only it were just Mohand! For it is one thing to have a sole confidant, a sole companion, a sole lover—and something else entirely when everyone, absolutely everyone, heedlessly invites themselves into your head, thoughts, and most private parts of your body. Yes, hell is others. Others are a permanent revulsion.

She picked up the poor crumpled jacket with her fingers and moved it out of view, then wiped her hands with a clean handkerchief. She could now get back to her dress, which she had just set aside.

IV

Nine thirty. She had overslept again. For six years she had struggled to fight off sleep. Late or painful morning awakenings, long naps no shorter than three hours, and—the ultimate sign of her defeated will—unexpectedly nodding off during bus rides, even though, distrustful by nature, she had always disdained people who slept in public spaces.

Why did she enjoy sleep so much? Surely it was the only time she had for herself, when she could at last savor solitude—the real kind—and forget Mohand and the others. Sleep chased the ghosts away. But she had always like to sleep, even when she was young, even before what she vaguely referred to— perhaps out of modesty—as the *Problem*.

However, she had to get up, since she had a bus to catch; Tizi awaited her. She slowly got ready, already anticipating the irritation and the possible nausea that would be brought on by the ugly crowd of mustached *flâneurs* and veiled women passing by. The hostile or perverted stares from the former. The whistling and high-pitched voices from the latter. The bus drivers' nasal and monotone voices, which were just as irritating: repeating, like a supplication, their destinations. And then there were the buses themselves: dirty, loud, and seemingly straight out of the past century and survivors of some sad war from which their seats and passengers' faces often seemed to carry the scars. Sometimes, though, they did not just "seem to." This war that had refused to say its name for a whole decade had really and truly taken place. A war that pitted wild-eyed, thickly bearded zealots against an entire grieving nation; a war that slit everyone's throats, even those of newborn babies, to staunch the inextinguishable red thirst of a barbarous and sadistic divinity invented by pious demons.

But Tizi—Tizi, where she was headed and where Warda lived—had also had other wars and other battles. Battles she,

Chahira, had never experienced. In April of 1980, it was El Moudja's sea breeze that rocked the barely two-year-old little girl that she was; and in 1998, when the whole of Kabylia's capital was under the reign of burning tires and tear gas, she had been gone for two years. Back then, she barely knew the singer who had been murdered and whose death sparked the whole region's wrath.* In high school, her boarding-school classmates talked about other musicians and sang other songs: love songs that made the rough teenage girls cry.

She had nothing but disdain for her classmates, who had filled out, who were already completely done with childhood, and for their language, which she sometimes found to be bold, while she was still thin and kept the limpid gaze of innocence. But she still remembered the stupid songs that stirred them, and she caught herself humming them every now and then. She knew deep down that the young singer her classmates dreamed about was far from talentless, but she had long been taught to distrust everything that was too Kabyle. Later, as she grew, she started to distrust the country as a whole and everything it could produce, which did not amount to much. Kabyle or "Arab," they were all the same, with their fat and deformed bodies, their worn-out clothes, their dusty streets, their mindsets that were just as dusty, their prohibitions, and their moldering and reeking imaginations. In El Moudja, they were all like that; but in Tizi N'Tlelli, she recognized that some were beautiful: they read, argued, wanted to be open-minded. These ones found grace in her eyes.

The same artist who made the boarding-school girls of Lalla Zineb go crazy in the 1990s mourned the Singer-Hero's death in the very bus that happened to carry her toward Tizi in the summer of 2001. Aired nonstop, the heartbreaking words came to her:

Semḥeɣ-ak imeṭṭawen-iw
Semḥeɣ ay nehqeɣ fell-ak

* The Kabylian singer Lounès Matoub was assassinated in 1998. Matoub was an advocate for Berber rights in Algeria.—*Trans.*

Yewwet useffud di leɛmer-iw
Makken ḍralleɣ ɣef lǧetta-k*

Then:

Ayen yakk yerɣan ass-nni
Di Tubiret, Bgayet, Tizi
Ur telli d tiselbi
Seg wulawen i d-teffeɣ tmes†

Tizi was burning once again. Its tires, its state institutions, its movie theater—everything burned. And, just as in 1998, stones were thrown from one side and from the other, tear gas again and forever. Tear gas, but also bullets—real bullets. Both sides stopped, however, when a young woman passed by. The young protesters, in particular, worried that they would be mistaken for thugs. This was why the stones had stopped flying as she passed through.

"Go ahead, miss." They still called her miss back then. That was seventeen years ago.

A young man passing by handed her a tissue. "Here. This will help a little with the tear gas. If I were you, I'd go that way around. Stay safe."

Yet, not everything was as chivalrous in that "war." Stories were told about the gendarmes committing the very worst of disgraceful acts in the villages. That they burst into peoples' homes day and night under the most banal of pretexts, that they

---

* I forgive you my tears
I forgive you my sobs
And my pierced soul
When I saw your lifeless body.
This excerpt is from the song "Xas akka tɣabed" ("In Spite of Your Disappearance"), written and performed by Hacène Ahrès in honor of the singer Lounès Matoub, killed in 1998.
† Everything that burned on that day
In Bouira, Béjaïa, and Tizi-Ouzou
Showed not insanity:
The fire arose from hearts.

harassed the men and took too many liberties with the women. Truth or unbridled imagination? Malika, Warda's older sister, had promised her that all of it was true; moreover (this is well known), there is no smoke without fire . . . What was for certain was that everywhere in this bloodied Kabylia young people died from the police's very real bullets. More than a hundred. Wasn't this why she had wanted to come? Malika and Warda's brother had been wounded. From detour to detour, from rioters' slogans to gendarmes' uniforms, she had at last arrived at the hospital to listen to this newly eighteen-year-old protestor tell the story of how he had braved bullets and taunted the gendarmes, yelling at the top of his voice his "rejection of oppression and the arbitrary." "No forgiveness," he continued to chant from bed.

His life was no longer in danger, but he no doubt received what was a fatal blow a few months later, when he learned that the leaders of the *Iderman* movement, as it was called, had "negotiated" with the state. The end of hostilities against the locals and distributing business permits to the idle youth, who were no doubt close to the negotiator. Too bad for the dead.

A hand—that of the man in his forties sitting next to her on the bus—suddenly brushed against her; she was brutally pulled from her thoughts. The hand in question then dove straight between the person's legs. Here was another guy who scratched between his thighs. This act was going to torture her for the rest of the day. They did this on purpose, every single one of them. To provoke her—and also to get the feeling of touching her. That was the impression she had. She looked at him, a storm in her eyes.

V

Among the few young women she counted as friends, Warda, with her sweet face and slender frame, was the only one who could model the outfit Chahira was going to show in Vienna. Beautiful women did not run, neither literally or figuratively, through the streets near the seamstress's home; the few "roses" she did know were, for the most part, veiled and would not under any circumstances have accepted the job she was offering.[*]

Her *hubris*—is this not what they said about her, that she was too proud?—sometimes whispered that she should just do it herself. Just a few years ago this might have been possible; but the mirror—again the mirror—showed her that this was no longer the case. Though it reflected all her charm, it also reminded her that the laws of gravity had asserted themselves. Anyway, it would not make for a good impression: she being both the designer and the model. People would accurately sense this pride, seeing it more clearly than she did, making her unpleasant in their eyes and them hostile in hers.

No, Warda would do a fine job. She imagined this long-haired, delicate-featured redhead in the outfit Chahira would get into the finals. She considered this outfit for the nth time before heading toward Tizi, and her verdict was summed up in one word: "Elegant! Elegant!"

At first, she was annoyed by the requirement "that all entries in the competition be inspired by traditional clothing from the participants' respective countries." Arg! Pompous and grotesque words, just like the word *tradition* itself. A word that people in her own country used every hour of every day; she had wound up hating it. Fine. This competition was not for her. Vienna's loss! But then ideas gradually stitched together in

[*] In Arabic, the name *Warda* signifies "rose."—*Trans.*

her mind. A straight mid-length skirt with thin red and black stripes inspired by the *fouta*.* An oversized cropped black top, flared sleeves, also mid-length but trimmed with fringe similar to an *amendil*.† A long coral pendant—red, obviously, to match the skirt. That was it. As for the shoes, she would forgo tradition. Sober, though lightly polished, high heels would tie it all together.

How could she have believed, when she first started sewing, that the outfits she would create would qualify her for the finals of an international fashion design competition? She had not intended to join this trade. When she was eighteen years old, her parents decided that she had had enough—if not too much—education and pulled her from school. They then had to find some sort of trade for her. Because, of course, it was out of the question for this strange and intolerable girl to be also a financial burden. For that matter, hers was not really the type of home to support family members in need. So what should be chosen for her? An internship with a hairdresser? Chahira was gripped with nausea at the very thought of the long hours she would have to spend standing there, listening to stupid chitchat from all the housewives with bleached hair, who were just as fat as they were meddlesome—who, with admirable imagination, would enumerate their mother-in-laws' faults, their brazen sister-in-laws' scandals, and their husbands' business revenues, either downplaying or truly inflating the numbers, depending on whether they sought to inspire compassion or envy. They would, of course, ask her why she did not have one: a husband. Some would recommend that she be more cunning; others would tell her—with sympathetic looks worthy of the greatest tragedies—not to despair, as everything was but *mektoub*.‡ And she might tolerate their idiotic twaddle at first, but sooner or later she would wind up shooting daggers at them: this always made her appear even more disagreeable, but it reduced everyone to silence.

---

* *Fouta*: A long piece of fabric with vertical red and black stripes, knotted around the waist and worn on top of the Kabyle dress.

† The *amendil* is a fringed scarf, often black and/or yellow, traditionally worn by Kabyle women.

‡ *Mektoub*: An Arabic word that in Islam signifies "destiny."—*Trans.*

Thankfully, her parents—for they were the ones who should really decide, isn't that right?—quickly changed their minds. Not because Chahira would not be happy in this profession; that was of little consequence, was it not? Anyway, could this dull and grouchy girl—in the eyes of whom nothing and no one ever found favor—find happiness anywhere? No, it was just that being a hairdresser did not offer much on the financial front. For how many women in the tiny village of El Moudja were going to set foot in a beauty salon now that the area's new masters had decreed that the only kind of hair allowed was the shaggy beards adorning their own chins?

This was, and rightly so, another reason for not sending Chahira off to style hair. The only hairdresser in El Moudja was about five hundred meters from the family home, and their senseless and exhausting daughter obstinately refused to cover her head when she went out. Pure madness in those times, when heads were, in fact, cut off under the slightest pretext and strewn pretty much everywhere along the country's roads. The only solution was to keep her inside as much as possible. Hence the internship as a seamstress: *Khalti* Nouara—the old woman who was supposed to teach her the tricks of the trade—lived in the same building, just two floors below. How practical.*

Chahira still remembered the first day of her internship. Out of defiance, out of spite, she had made it a point of honor to annoy the kindly old lady: to ignore her advice, to do everything wrong. Not that she had to try very hard: she was distracted by nature and was even more hapless with her hands. But Nouara ended up winning her over . . . well, at least a little bit. She succeeded more than anyone else had, in any case. By not making a special effort in this area—or, at least, by not showing that she was. The old seamstress respected her apprentice's silences, smiling with indulgence at her clumsiness and pretending not to notice her flagrant lack of goodwill. And, miracle of miracles, that young girl who enjoyed nothing and nobody grew to like the old neighbor lady. It was that Nouara was just so nice! Little by little, what started as drudgery became something enjoyable; and if her apprentice's hands remained a bit bumbling

---

* *Khalti* signifies "aunt" in Arabic.—*Trans.*

and slow, the work they accomplished increasingly delighted her teacher.

And more importantly, Chahira became progressively aware that there she possessed a new way of allowing her creativity free rein. This time without danger. Yes, she was now creating differently. She designed long dresses with side slits. Frilly shirts. Plunging necklines. "Daring" clothes that women still found a way to wear, thanks to parties where they danced alone, free from the eyes of the men who celebrated in the courtyard, drinking in full breaths of fresh air. Thanks to, sometimes, a sudden bold desire to please a husband who was strict about his wife's morality, but sometimes—and only sometimes—happy that she had thought about pleasing his eyes and male sensibilities. So, in the end, these bits of fabric she fashioned together were not all that different from the lines of verse from more than twenty years ago . . . But words are always the most dangerous and the most feared, as Mr. Rouha would say.

VI

Back in Tizi N'Tlelli, the city made of flowers and thorns, just like the gorse bushes that symbolized it. Ever since its revolts had been quelled, this city long perfumed with tear gas and burning tires smelled only of the garbage that shamelessly spilled from the public trash cans. The stench of rotting organic matter assaulted each breath. Chahira panicked, moving her nose to different parts of her body and taking in sharp sniffs of her skin. No, it was not her; it was not because of last night's indigestion. The trash cans smelled. She could relax.

Her ears, however, were greeted with pleasant sounds. A CD vendor was playing one of the songs by the singer-hero who had been treacherously murdered in the summer of 1998. She inaudibly hummed the tune, trying to remember the lyrics. Alas, the Kabyle was too formal for her, daughter of El Moudja.

This was why she loved this city. Everywhere else she went, she heard only the coarse voices of passersby who exchanged jokes delivered with such violence they resembled threats. Sometimes an obscenity was spit out in her wake. She would turn around, face flushed, and return it in a low voice; or she would hurry her step, wounded—the word had been cast out for her; it was she who had unwittingly provoked it.

Yes, ugly words, vulgar words—you would hear them a little everywhere. That was permissible. But music, God save us! Was the call to prayer not enough? Was it not one of the most beautiful songs? Music, that Devil's purr, was banished. In every street she knew. Except for those in Tizi N'Tlelli. Hence her joy at passing through them. Now that she thought of it, she needed to buy something at that video store: she was looking for *Love and Revenge,* the film where the sublime Asmahan sang "Layali El Uns fi Vienna." She wanted to feel Vienna, breathe Vienna, dream about Vienna before going there for real. And she especially wanted to watch all the beautiful actresses waltz. But the shopkeeper did not know the film. He did not even know the song; he had her repeat the title twice. It was true that people in Tizi were not obsessed with Asmahan. That said, who still knew about the film? She probably would not find it anywhere.

Ammi Amar's shop was a bit farther away, right in front of the Lalla Zineb high school. She absolutely had to go buy the tulle she had not been able to get the last time as she had almost fled the store, panicking over the unfurling odors she believed to be her own. Amar the Aesthete would again tell her the story of how his wife, deceased for seventeen years now, had taught him to make dolls out of tulle. He would tell her again how they kept him company ever since that fateful day he lost his Ouiza.

It was Sister Bernadine who had taught his wife to make the tulle figurines. They were clever, those Sœurs Blanches; they had a way of serving the colonial cause while getting the local population to love them* . . . And their savoir faire! People still said that those who had been educated by this community of missionaries had had proper schooling, that they knew how to do everything. This had been Ouiza's case. With pride, the Aesthete talked about what a good housekeeper she was and how clean she kept the home. He would recall with nostalgia how her crystalline voice filled the air with beautiful songs as she worked. And he would close his story by reminding Chahira how idiotic Ouiza's death was—she who had always sparkled with intelligence—all because of a stray bullet let loose during an altercation between the gendarmes and young protesters. Elsewhere in the country, the senseless string of deaths had actually slowed. Heads had stopped being cut off; the bloody savagery that decimated entire villages was thought to be extinguished. And then, then, it was the young Kabyles' turn to

---

* The Sœurs Blanches, or Sœurs Missionnaires de Notre-Dame d'Afrique, were a group of female missionaries who, from this order's initial work in Algiers in the late 1860s, worked primarily with women and children. They engaged in several areas: education, religious teachings, and health-related fields. The Sœurs Blanches were not active only in Algiers; they settled in different locations throughout the country, including Kabylia.—*Trans.*

fall to the murderous bullets of those who were supposed to be fighting the killers . . .

*

"Ouiza died with them; her soul was young like theirs!" concluded Ammi Amar sadly. Chahira had listened to him tell his wife's story three or four times, but always with the same tenderness for this old aesthete. He was loyal to a woman's memory in a country where few men could tolerate being a widower—where they could remarry less than a month after losing the one who was supposed to be their other half. Mohand also listened to the story, sharing the widower's pain, but he also grew irritated by the numerous repetitions. And now, he mumbled his sympathy and gratitude, for by listening so patiently to the old man, Chahira earned one of his figurines. She promised to take very good care of it, then purchased two meters of tulle and left, full of her invisible companion's silent clamors.

VII

"Come look at what your daughter's got in her school note-books!"

And the father recited out loud:

My body next to yours, I'll become a cat
And purr contentedly
As these arms that indulge me
Hold me tighter yet

"You see what she's reading—the one you sent off to school! Oh, and it is lovely, her education. Now you see why she always has her nose stuck in a book! And they call that great poetry. The poetry of sin and shame is more like it!"

The mother, who had only a cursory knowledge of French, moaned, face in her hands, asking God what she had done to deserve such a daughter, a shame of this sort, while her husband paced in and out of the living room, striking the floor with his belt, which had grown limp from the unrelenting blows it had dealt the culprit. In spite of the red marks streaking his daughter's martyred body, his anger had not subsided. He would have liked to whip her again and again, but he had stopped as soon as blood began dripping from her thin, assailed arm. Then he had begun to sob, stunned by the violence he had displayed.

In the days that followed the beating, he waited on her hand and foot, dressing with the utmost gentleness the high school student's wounds with alcohol and hydrogen peroxide. But his decision was made: his daughter had studied enough. It was time for her to return home and help in the domestic tasks with her mother—this mother who was so distraught that she had, for a few days, forgotten to yell at everyone.

Chahira's hand mechanically ran over her body as she remembered the abuse she had endured that day. She again felt the pain they had inflicted upon her and that was revived each time they tended to her. She thought she would die from the wounds. She did not die; she was not even hospitalized, as that would have put everyone in a state of shame—and the torturer would have been in a tough spot. The scars disappeared little by little, and the physical suffering vanished, leaving behind only pride. Yes, it was pride: her writing had been mistaken for the works of great poets! All this savagery for a poem they had believed was copied from a book! What would she have suffered if she had confessed that she had written the lines?

"Yes, it was mine, this beautiful poem." She smiled, the very idea filling her with pride. Then other verses, all born beneath her pen, came back to her, out of order, approximately:

Follow the lines of this body
Exhausted by such constraint
Bridled by a thousand years of modesty
And who wants you ever yet

And:

He murmurs a thousand melodies
His arms sing a thousand caresses
O sweet bliss
Take me to paradise!

Her body suddenly burned beneath these fiery words. She looked around. No, this time it was nobody's fault. It was just she who had caught fire with these racy words. How had she been able to write such words when she had not yet turned eighteen? She almost understood her father's rage.

But her fever was already contaminating the others. Soon, barely audible sighs would climb up from the depths of the men and women who brushed her body while she walked past Lalla Zineb, the high school where she had spent three years. Agitated hands would once again move, furtively or brazenly, up to the excited places between their legs. A voice resembling

Mohand's already mumbled in irritation. "She never gives us a single moment of rest, that one," the voice seemed to say.

*

She had only one good memory from her three years of being a boarding student at that high school/prison: the library. Pages secretly skimmed while waiting for a teacher who was late, whole books devoured during the long hours of studying when her classmates attempted to confront the most formidable mathematics and physics problems. She discovered Stendhal, despising his Julien Sorel and admiring Fabrice del Dongo; she was both fascinated and bothered by Hamlet's philosophical hesitations, and she pitied his sweet fiancée, Ophelia; she was indignant at the horrible end of Emma Bovary, a gracious and intelligent woman whose only fault was to refuse ennui and mediocrity.

But also: How many flavorless and inedible meals, lukewarm soups in which insects and every sort of body hair floated; how many sticky tables upon which only the most foolhardy dared rest their hands or arms; how many plates and cups made from gluey plastic; how many after-school snacks of bread so stale it would shatter teeth, and chocolate that was just as brittle? How much rushing so as not to miss out on these haphazard snacks? How many disparaging remarks from the monitors, who were sometimes overly zealous about a poorly made bed, a stray hair that had remained in the sink, or a prolonged whisper after ten o'clock at night—the time when all the boarders were supposed to have found Morpheus? How many calls to order because of a distracted glance out the window, a laugh that was a little too loud, a dress that wasn't long enough . . . ? In that all-girl high school, they showed an almost laughable amount of concern for the students' morality. They ensured that they had no other interests apart from their studies, that they had no male visitors, that they did not dream of romance. But young girls of sixteen will always be young girls of sixteen, even in the worst of prisons. Some of her classmates wept while humming the sultry refrains of beautiful young men beginning their careers in music, others wore languorous looks and sometimes even made brazen allusions to their young male English or physics teachers, whom they secretly dreamed of marrying. And she—she whom every girl said was serious and irreproachable—who was she thinking about when she wrote her smoldering lines?

Chahira nervously bit her lower lip as a slightly blurred distant image of a young man approached. He must have been barely twenty years old and was accompanied by an older gentleman whom he helped with odd electrical or painting jobs: some sort of apprentice handyman, no doubt promised to a mundane future of hard labor and difficult months' ends that would only be softened by his own image: that of a carefree Apollo who was also something of a dreamer. As she looked again at his small, delicate face, which contrasted with his robust athlete's body, faint grumblings came to her—from where she did not know. Mohand, Nacer, and the others again. A *merqouchette* gave a snide laugh. But she chose to ignore it.

My body next to yours, I'll become a cat
And purr contentedly
As these arms that indulge me
Hold me tighter yet

Yes, these were beautiful lines! And in remembering them, she felt proud at having written them. At having held her own at that sad school where dreams and laughter were forbidden. Where all they did was perpetuate the insidious warnings that had already been beaten into their students since they were children. Beware of anyone with short hair! Of those lazy and pretentious creatures made of hair, muscle, and—most especially—unclean thoughts! Do not dream about them, do not love them, and—most importantly—do not go near them! Watch out for their sweet words; keep away from their soft whispers and caresses!

These injunctions had an afflicting banality; all the girls of her generation had been privy to them in a more-or-less veiled way. Blessed were those adventurers, the reckless, the disobedient women! She was too good a girl, almost shy, and did not take part in any of that. In forty years of life, she had never known those furtive caresses and those stolen kisses made so famous by artists throughout the world. Oh, that was nothing exceptional! For all young girls afraid of being considered debauched, these joys were only accessible once married—that is to say, in finding oneself at the mercy of an egotistical husband and intolerable children, for whom they would have to do the housekeeping and cooking and dispense a thousand kindnesses each God-given day. All of this while complaining and growing irritated as little as possible, as that could risk their reputations as domestic angels and possibly even their statuses as wives. In short, in this country—and maybe elsewhere too—a woman's life was limited to three possible choices: whore, slave, or nun. Right or wrong, the last one seemed to her to be the least insulting.

But if people said she was good, it was only because they had never been privy to her abundant imagination. The nun she had been knew how to dream up forbidden acts and even to sing them in the manner of great poets. She had had her hour of rebellion, and she was proud of it. One single regret: she should have screamed at those wretched school wardens who had confiscated her writings, then at her parents whom they had called in, telling them that these poems had not been copied from anywhere; that they were hers, and that she had placed all her desire and talent into them.

But then she arrived at Warda's. She was going to love the *fouta*-skirt and the *amendil*-top. The black would contrast beautifully with her alabaster skin, and the skirt's red would accentuate her flaming russet hair. As Chahira rang the doorbell, she confidently told herself that with such a svelte and graceful model, she had every chance of winning.

VIII

It is well known that ghosts grow bolder at night. At night, they breach the diktat of consciousness and dance brazenly in the darkness that sometimes dares to defy the feeble moonlight shining through the blinds. Their farandoles, at once solemn and tormented, split from the hushed comfort where weary spirits hope to find respite. They impudently open imagination's doors—hailing down memories, anguish, and bad instincts—and welcome this handsome assemblage to their party.

It was one in the morning. Chahira had been arguing with Nacer's sister for almost an hour. Ever since that magical night when this young man of rare finesse enveloped her in flowers and tenderness, ever since he deployed romanticism's unexpected treasures that eventually culminated in charnel beatitude—ever since that night, Kenza no longer concealed her jealousy. What she feared was her brother becoming forever infatuated with her, the neighbor with supernatural powers; the neighbor whose spirit communed, from afar, with the others' thoughts, deciphering their voiceless groans and unearthing their intentions. It was out of the question for Nacer to marry this girl who was just as odd as she was arrogant; she could not have a worse sister-in-law. Plus, she was much older than him. So, to intimidate her neighbor, Kenza laughed. Her laughter was hard, contemptuous and goading, while Chahira, in a fury, silently cursed her; and Nacer, exasperated by them both, expressed his complete irritation through repeated interjections.

"*Din djeddek*,"* she suddenly said. Because Kenza had just furtively pushed on her lower belly, Chahira felt the muscles of her intimate parts relax, then a strong smell of urine and sweat emanated from her body. The neighbor chuckled, while she,

---

* This insult literally means "May your grandfather's religion be cursed."

unable to swallow her humiliation, attempted to retaliate. The enemy also had to lose control and give off the same smell of urine. But Kenza held firm and parried each attack, while her laughter became ever less assured.

Once again, Chahira fought the feeling of shame that rushed over her with each strange smell that escaped her body against her will. A stench of urine, like today, but also that of sweat, gas, clotted blood, vomit, onions, fish, rotten eggs, and so many other things that were just as nauseating as they were perplexing. And, once again, she felt her own weakness, her lack of capacity to defend herself. Why could the others hold back their odors when she tried to force them to let go? Why were they always vigilant and effective while she always fell prey to them? Why did she lack the reflexes, the comeback?

Soon Nacer was not the only one who was bothered. More and more voices were raised, railing against the incessant complaining. First, Mohand uttered impatient exclamations, begging her to be "silent." Then from everywhere, the others started to grumble.

"What do you all want from me?" she screamed in her head at everyone.

Then they grew more upset. Sniggers fired from all around. Thousands of invisible fingers started touching her. The anger grew increasingly male: flush with an invasive desire. With sighs that were more or less discreet. With numerous invitations, either romantic or threatening. With bouquets of flowers, caresses, and even obscene gestures.

"You disgust me! Do you hear me? You only have one thing on your mind!"

She rolled over in bed; now she was vexed.

"Sick perverts! Leave me alone!"

Someone punched her in the eye. This was followed by a lustful man's panting; at once he seized her body.

"Punching!" She lashed out sarcastically, "How romantic!"

And suddenly she felt sad. She asked herself why, in her country, men were almost all abrupt, violent even, in their approach to intimate relationships. Ever since she began suffering through this strange experience of mental contact with the others, it was a rare few who ventured tenderness or refinement to tempt her body and senses. Sure, they had not been brought up this way; neither had she for that matter. But was there not something of an innate savoir faire for this type of thing? Can they not just know the necessary gestures and words?

Her bed suddenly started to creak beneath the passionate movements a mysterious lover inflicted upon her. Suddenly, a tickling in her lower body and a slight pain. Then, little by little, a growing sensation of pleasure. Plenitude, ecstasy. Everything was calmer, happier; she slept serenely in the arms of this new lover.

IX

Not every night ended so peaceably, however. How long had it taken before she gave in to all those male temptations? To finally accept the pleasure procured by an exquisite lover, how much reticence, how many scruples, battles, tears?

Those sleepless nights spent evading the touch of these satyrs she did not see! Well, only the *others* did not see; Chahira saw them. She saw their bulky and repulsive shadows, their unkind and sometimes grimacing faces. The best ones were those who were young and healthy. Sometimes they had hairy bodies that were paunchy and greasy, or toothless mouths with bad breath. These moved libidinously and had vicious laughs; and they disgusted her the most. When one of their crude hands brushed her skin, she leapt from bed with a stifled shriek. She hurriedly moved to the other side of the bed—it was a "bed for two" that her "folks," who had bought a new one, no longer wanted. But other hands, other greedy bodies were always waiting for her. Where could she run, where could she run? She dragged her pillow, blanket, and tired body, which was always alert, to each corner of the room in hopes of finding a haven, a quiet spot where she would be out of reach. Then, often, at the end of a night of wandering and wearisome panic, sleep got the better of her and all these neighbors who invaded her body and mind, beleaguering her mentally. She slept, at last calmed.

Of course, it would have been different if there were only one single ghost, only one single admirer, only one single lover. Oh, to find each night familiar tender words, the same loving arms, their caresses, and the delicious quiver of flesh that follows! She would have thanked the heavens for such a blessing. Instead, she suffered the daily nightmare of being owned by several hands, sometimes several bodies. And she became nothing more than an endless nausea. The nausea of having her whole body assaulted and enduring being touched by all these strange bodies; the nausea of not knowing how to defend herself, of feeling like a vulgar slut, like the most common of whores; and especially the nausea of telling herself that for all these male ghosts who desired her, she was undoubtedly nothing more than that . . .

And then she gave in. Too much fighting, too much anguish, too many sleepless nights . . . So, on a night many long months after the Problem had begun, she decided to get into bed, relax, ignore all the satyrs, and never again run from them . . . She didn't succeed at first; she continued to panic in spite of herself when she saw the graying mustaches and potbellied hairy bodies. Then, suddenly, a handsome apparition: a svelte and strong body and a young man's striking face—he was undoubtedly younger than she. At the time, she was almost thirty-five years old, while this handsome neighbor, whom she had never actually met, had to be thirty. No more than thirty-two. And it was good, so very good to finally stop resisting. To let herself get carried away by his soft murmurs; to let herself be possessed by those arms that were so strong yet so gentle. Yes, happiness was abandoning herself to him, belonging entirely to him, discovering with him the ecstatic triumph of the flesh and ending the evening in his arms.

But this was not possible. The others—always and forever the others—did not want this. It started with the jealous *merqouchettes,* who disrupted their affectionate games with wicked laughter; the other young men were also jealous. And there was no end to their groaning.

Mohand was among the jealous; his dreadful mood made this all too clear. He grumbled, too, taking on a contrite tone: the tone of someone who had been betrayed. And yet he had lost interest in her a long time ago—he had stopped trying to get close to her and grew angry when she spoke sweetly to him. He wanted her to leave him alone; he did not want to be part of the group who tortured her, caused her anguish, and then made her feel guilty. She had only been his once, when he had appeared with an almost violent arousal. She hated him for it, and he hated himself for it too. Since then, he either tried to ignore her or to make an enormous effort at self-control when temptation grew too strong. No, he clearly did not want to be "her man"; anyway, she was not his type, this girl who lacked Kabyle simplicity and good sense. Then why his current crisis?

"Mohand, why are you making such a fuss?"

His grunts seemed to say that she had betrayed him; that she had found pleasure and solace, while he, on the other hand, was alone.

"You know full well you are my favorite, Mohand."

And this was true; she cared a lot for Mohand. He was sympathetic to her sorrow; he understood her suffering. Even when he rejected her, he did it in part for her; he did not want to participate in her unhappiness. And most importantly—and something she would always remember—there was the way this simple, yet tenderhearted, young man had suddenly and gently touched her arm to console her while she wept, recalling the cruel words her father had beaten into her: that she was a worthless piece of shit, that she meant less than nothing. Yes, Mohand had calmly consoled her that night. It was one of those numerous dark days, one of those interminable insults she would endure over and over again, since the Problem—her accursed malady—had settled in for good.

X

"Where were you, you wretched seed? Where've you been hiding all this time? O my God, my God, what did I do to have such a calamity?"

The mother, arms raised to the sky, reeled off her endless lamentations, while Chahira, wan and despondent, slowly closed the front door. It was almost four in the afternoon; she had left at seven-thirty in the morning, while everyone else was still asleep.

"Answer me, misfortune's daughter, answer!" The mother, exasperated by her silence, seized her by the arm.

"It's my birthday!" Chahira quickly shouted. "I still have the right to go out for a bit on my birthday! I was in Tizi N'Tlelli."

Her voice wavered, and she burst into tears.

Her mother panicked. She noticed the young woman's despondency and pallor. She immediately let go of her arm and slowly murmured, "It doesn't look like you had much fun . . ."

"Leave me alone. You completely forgot my birthday . . ."

She walked to her bedroom, overcome with tears, and quietly shut the door.

The mother was stunned. There was no way she would be crying because they had forgotten her birthday! Since when had anyone in this family remembered one? This was grotesque, almost laughable, a spoiled child's fancy. Then, she was suddenly gripped with fear: this birthday was clearly not the reason for the hysteria—Chahira had to be hiding something. At once she covered her face, frenetically repeating, "My God, take pity on us." For she seemed to have guessed what had happened. In her crude and tainted imagination, which resembled that of many fellow citizens of her age and condition, there was just one little thing that could provoke this level of distress for a woman: a serious, unpardonable error that only death could cleanse.

She burst into her daughter's room.

"What did you do? You miserable wretch!"

She leaned over the bed where her prone daughter was completely still, as if stunned, and grabbed her by the hair. She met no resistance. Chahira gave a feeble groan of pain, then crouched in fear at the foot of the bed. Rabéa's panic grew, for her daughter was not the type of person to allow herself to be mistreated without reacting. She quickly pulled back her hand and ventured a hypocritical pat on her devastated daughter's head. Her daughter looked up, eyes pleading, almost happy; and by some miracle, something softened the heart of this old woman who, in forty years of motherhood, had never known how to offer her children anything but endless complaining. The swirl of suffering and fright she perceived in her daughter—an arrogant girl who normally was so good at hiding her feelings— overwhelmed her. In order for Chahira Lahab to reveal so much pain, her misfortune had to be truly significant.

Rabéa's voice was infinitely soft when, now caressing Chahira's hair with greater sincerity, she asked what was wrong.

"What is it, my daughter, why all this pain? Talk to your mother, Chahira, there's nothing to fear."

The words fell painfully from the daughter's lips: "I'm sick, Mama, very sick." And she started to cry.

Two affectionate arms, those of a woman for whom maternal love had without warning just awoken after a forty-year slumber, wrapped her up, while comforting words asked her what this illness was, all the while assuring her that everything would be fine.

The name of the illness fell like an ax. A form of psychosis. Of course the old woman did not know what it was, so it had to be explained. It had to be explained that her daughter had hallucinations that impacted all of her senses. That she heard voices, laughter. That she smelled all sorts of extraordinary odors she thought were her own. That she thought people far away were touching her, that they attacked her modesty, that they did worse things—all from a distance.

Now it was Rabéa's turn to be devastated. She slowly moved away from her daughter. The tenderness that had been magically born inside of her disappeared just as mysteriously as it had arrived. Something hostile filled her gaze. She almost wanted to shake Chahira, to grab her by the hair once more. In the end, only one thing was for certain: her daughter was mad; and what could anyone expect from an insane daughter apart from shame and dishonor?

She did not utter a word; though within, she returned to her lamentations: "My God, my God, where will I now hide? Where will I hide my shame?" A semblance of compunction kept her from shouting all her fury out at her daughter. For when had this strange girl, who had, at her core, always been slightly crazy, ever been a source of pride? Rabéa had tolerated her clumsiness, her laziness, her incompetent housework, her mood swings, her stubbornness . . . And how did she reward her? By inflicting upon her the ultimate humiliation.

She quickly left the bedroom without saying a word, without any concern for her daughter, who was now crying in silence.

*

That was six years ago. She never told her mother what had happened in Tizi N'Tlelli—as that was indeed where she had gone. She did not tell her about the long, agonizing hours on the bus where everyone seemed to be laughing at her confusion; where the lunatic seated next to her smothered her entire body through his very presence, then overwhelmed her with the unbearable stench of chewing tobacco and bad breath, smells she gradually felt become her own. Then, triumphant and free of the foulness he had foisted on her, he made a show of holding his nose, acting disgusted by this woman who smelled bad.

She did not talk with her about her astonishment when, once at the doctor's, she found six other people waiting their turn. She thought psychiatrists' waiting rooms were always empty; but people visibly feared for their minds where chaos reigned, just as it did throughout the entire country. She did not talk with her about the painful tears that had accompanied the story of her hallucinations, fears, and exhaustion. Or about the word *psychosis,* which fell like a weighty and perhaps eternal condemnation. Or about that medication, whose scribbled name on a prescription pad was already humiliating.

She did not tell her about the previous night's horrors. About the ghost who had their young neighbor's face and voice. A young neighbor who spied her thoughts. Who gasped when she "said" something smart and who laughed at her foolishness. Who followed her wherever she went. Who shot her voyeuristic glances and issued half-joyous, half-annoyed chuckles when she changed into her nightshirt. She had turned off the light, thinking she would be invisible if she undressed in the dark; but she had continued to feel his eyes on her, and the short laughter did not stop.

Then there were other faces, other ghosts. The whispers, the cries, the whistles. How many thousands of voices besieged her? There were not yet any hands, but they would come soon enough. Wandering hands, caressing hands, violent hands. But the worst, the worst, were the thoughts to which these unwelcome guests had access. More than that of her body, it was the raping of her mind and thoughts that was the most unbearable. Her most private thoughts falling into the open!

She tried to ignore them, to think of more concrete things, more "normal" things. About what she was going to do the next day. Deliver two dresses to a client. Tidy up her armoire. And then go to the bank to withdraw a little money. It has been so long since she had stepped foot in there! She quickly visualized her debit card's pin number and immediately saw dozens of "heads" trying to memorize it. She was suddenly seized with dread: her neighbors hacked into her most intimate thoughts and now her passwords! She imagined her most closely guarded secrets passing from mouth to mouth and her bank account drained. She screamed in alarm.

XI

Since then, how many nightmares, how much worry, how many sensations of being spied upon, physically touched, defiled, humiliated? How many interminable nights spent fighting against demons, ghosts, and neighborhood men who attacked you from behind the walls, women neighbors who provoked you with sneers that were deafening in their silence? How many invisible virile spears pressed into her lower back and her femininity's charnel abysses?

Well, of course, there was the medication. At one point, she had agreed to take it; the nightmares had become too real, too overwhelming, too frightening. The doctor had told her that olanzapine was effective; it would treat all the symptoms. It would, of course, make her a bit drowsy, but that was nothing too concerning . . . Nothing too concerning, what a joke! It did not just make her drowsy—it had turned her into a zombie. A swollen and disfigured zombie. A heap of weight—she had gained almost ten kilos, without will or consciousness of doing so; a specter, a teetering sleepwalker with a dark tunnel disguised as a head. She spent interminable hours asleep, and when she woke up, she fell right back asleep. When she came to, she limped along, barely knowing where to go. Twice in a row she forgot her coat on the bus—to her mother's great dismay, for she sensed that the worst was yet to come. She lost her cell phone and could never remember where it might be. She could no longer concentrate on her sewing or housework, which she did less and less frequently. She almost stopped speaking. She could not stand herself any longer.

This went on for three months. Then she all at once decided to go off the medication. Why had she accepted this humiliating and dehumanizing course of treatment? It was not right for her, that much was clear. Anyway, was there a medication to address strange smells, general telepathy, and sensing touch from afar? Olanzapine was for those who *imagined* things, but she was not imagining things. Psychosis—oh, how this word terrified her—did not apply to her condition. After all, she had read up on psychotics. She knew they detached themselves from reality and their thoughts ran at countercurrents and were irrational. Was she detached from reality? Did she not go about her daily life in a somewhat normal way? Was she not logical and lucid? No, clearly she was not sick. She would never again take that accursed medicine.

Then, of course, she ceased to be a zombie. She became quite the opposite: a volcano in a constant state of eruption. Nearly every day was filled with arguments. On the bus, in the corner store, at the hairdresser, and—on the rare occasion—with clients.

"If you'd please step forward, Madame. People waiting."

What was it about these perfectly courteous words that could have sparked her fury? The woman she had asked to board the bus, the one hesitating outside the door, whirled around, her face bright red.

"Who are you to tell me what I should do? Why don't you get off your high horse and stop acting the queen."

"Why are you yelling like that? I didn't say anything inappropriate, you hysterical woman."

"I swear I'll crush, you pretentious little thing."

The "hysterical" woman had already grabbed her by the hair, saying over and over that she was going "to teach her a lesson." Chahira, out of her mind, scratched the hand that dared attack her face. Hands flew in to separate them, while scandalized voices whispered that women these days had neither good sense nor restraint—that the age of wisdom had passed.

"Completely crazy," whispered Chahira before sitting down.

Ever since she was diagnosed with psychosis, calling anyone she argued with "crazy" was particularly enjoyable. However, more often than not, she was the one who got called crazy. Sometimes indirectly, but barely concealed.

"Get in line, Madame, you have to get in line," she shouted at a fat lady who tried to cut ahead.

"You don't need to get in my face about it! We certainly have no shortage of crazy people right now."

This happened ten days ago at the vegetable seller's. She had barely absorbed the insult, when a man in his fifties with a vicious gaze touched her as he passed behind.

"You bastard, back off, why don't you!" She glared at him.

The man walked back toward her, threatening, "You'd better shut it before I disfigure you."

She faced him, furious and without an ounce of fear: "Disfigure me? Go try that with your wife or sister, why don't you. As for me, I'd advise you not to take one more step, for your own sake."

Silence fell. She felt as if she had won the respect of everyone there. Someone sympathetically said to her, "Calm yourself, Madame—he's not worth it!"

She was proud of this new wild temperament that knew no fear. Yet she felt helpless, without protection. Why did everyone think it all right to bully and assault her in this manner? Why did they speak rudely and besiege her? Could they sense this vulnerability hidden within her since childhood? This fear of others? Or was this perhaps her madness revealing itself in an insidious, unexplainable way, in spite of her normal appearance?

But did she really seem normal? Maybe she was the one who, without realizing it, was aggressive. And it was true that a voiceless rage tinged with anguish, a rage against the whole world, seemed to have been in her since the dawn of time. She felt it there, at the back of her throat almost all the time. But it was when she forgot about it that others seemed best able to sense it.

But her greatest anger, the one that never would diminish, the one that resentment would always awaken if it ever weakened, was with those who called themselves her family. "Families, I hate you," an artist or writer once said. She appropriated this phrase with the utmost conviction. What brilliant mind had penned it? Every time she tried to remember it, the letter K came to mind. She knew that that letter appeared more than once in that Czech writer's name; she had read a few excerpts of his writing when she was still in high school, but she now could barely recall his name. Yes, this line could only belong to that writer who had told the story of a young traveling clerk who metamorphosed into a cockroach.* Because that was full well what one became when declared psychotic, or in other words, insane: a miserable insect that is hunted down and crushed, who is not forgiven for the crime of continuing to live after the dishonorable transformation; after the fall from grace.

And so, just like this K's cockroach, everyone in that accursed home found ways to bother her, to provoke her. They taxed her nerves by constantly brushing past her, coming and going around her or, doing the opposite, standing close by and staying there for several minutes. She asked them to sit, but if they complied they did so while yelling at her, saying they had had enough of her insufferable reactions.

Of course, things did not always go so "well." Sometimes, their irritating milling around was too excruciating. She felt them touching her from afar, violating her body with only their thoughts, creating the strange and humiliating odors of urine, sweat, or cooked meals, and enjoying themselves all the while. She also heard their private snickering. So she panicked and tried to distance herself from these sensations with incoherent and unexpected gestures.

"What are you doing, misfortune's daughter? Now here you go making obscene gestures!"

The mother, who had just tossed out these words, grumbled something else under her breath. She placed her hand under her chin and turned her head, looking scandalized.

"She doesn't know what she's doing; she has lost her mind," the father jeered. "The poor thing is completely insane."

Were her parents really talking to her like this? How could they suggest she was making obscene gestures? And how dare they make fun of her illness? She felt the volcano within start to erupt. Her scream made the walls literally shake.

Everyone came running—the brother, the sister, the parents—and fell upon her. She tried to push them away, but they grabbed her wrists, overpowering her, and brought her to

* Chahira believes the phrase is from Franz Kafka, author of *The Metamorphosis*. In reality, it belongs to André Gide.

the ground. She tried to scream again; the father put his hand over her mouth.

"Shut it, *naal din yenmak.** You're making us the laughing-stock of our neighbors."

Yes, the neighbors, always and forever. The neighbors and what they might think; that was all that mattered, right? One could suffer terribly, agonize, die, but never proclaim one's suffering, all because of the *neighbors.*

Unexpectedly, she bit him. The others stepped in to free him. But he continued to hold her wrists. Exhausted from her useless struggle, she fell limp, powerless on the floor.

Her mother took advantage of this to bitterly deliver sharp blows to her head.

"Too spoiled! This one thinks she can do whatever she wants." And then more blows.

"Kader, are we really going to put up with this endless calamity? She has to be committed!"

"Yes," the father answered. "That's the only thing left to be done. We'll commit her."

They started backing away from her. She feebly yelled at them as they walked away. "You are crap! I hate you! You really are a great family!"

But they had already left the living room. Their voices reached her from the other room—they were calm, lighthearted even, as if nothing had happened. They had already moved on to something else.

She slowly got up. They had treated her as though she were obscene, destined to be committed. They had thrown her to the ground, beaten her, humiliated her. And at her age. Almost forty years old! Her proud soul bled, and she silently wept tears of defeat.

Then, from out of nowhere, Mohand emerged like a guardian angel. With infinite kindness, he placed a hand on her shoulder and uttered a few grunts she could not understand but that brought peace, a lot of peace to her weary mind. She smiled at the image of the slightly oafish, slightly awkward, and shy

* This insult, very common in Algeria, literally means "May your mother's religion be cursed."

young man. She tried to touch his hand to show her gratitude. But he stiffened and, frustrated, quickly went off. His annoyed grumbling came to her from the other side of the room.

Ever since then, Mohand was often there to console her after these frequent arguments. Once, when her sister had scratched her, they reproached her for doing the same back. When, after she had refused to switch rooms with her younger brother, her father contemptuously asked her who she thought she was, she who was "less than nothing and worth less than a piece of shit," expressions she often heard. Mohand would affectionately take her hand or clumsily dry her tears. And her smile returned. Her illness was no longer solely made up of nightmares; she had even come to appreciate it a little.

XII

The DVD of the Asmahan film was impossible to find; it was not for sale anywhere. But blessed be technology, could any song not just be downloaded from the internet? For days, Chahira listened to her song on repeat, and she happily sang the refrain:

Layali el uns fi Vienna
Nasimha min hawal el ganna
Nagham fi lgaww louhranna
Semeeha el tir baka ou ghanna

She was the bird. A bird held prisoner to morose daily routines, to a haunted loneliness, but to whom an imminent freedom was promised: a short-lived freedom called Vienna.

Freedom. There was a word she was not quite sure she understood. Of course, she had never been free. If she were, would she have remained one single minute longer among these people that she could not stand? Would she have continued to live with people who insulted her as often as they could and who had no interest in her suffering except for when it entertained them?

"Enough with that whining," said the male members of the family when she ventured to complain about her discomfort, "you don't seem in the least bit sick."

The mother added, "Oh, leave us be! If you are sick, it's just because you're spoiled and have a rotten character. And I think you cherish this misfortune; I think you enjoy it."

As for the sister, was it not true that each time they fought she said how happy she was that this had happened to her? That she could not wait to see her finish herself off, just as she often said she wanted to do? Had she not become her cruelest master, her cruelest source of trauma? She surpassed all the other minds with whom she communicated, as she had the power to hypnotize her, to control her actions, and to anticipate her intentions. She constantly felt her devising some plan to demean or make fun of her.

Any sense of goodness or calm instantly disappeared when that sister-demon showed up. At once, Chahira felt her body tremble or produce the most stomach-turning smells—often it was both. Sometimes it was the opposite: this sister's most private emanations invaded her nose and mouth. She felt her pungent body part on her lips and had to hold back her vomit. And when Chahira tried to retaliate, the master would try to paralyze her, to weaken her with one simple nod or flick of her finger. If that failed, she doused the psychotic woman's whole body in an acid with a smell that quickly dominated all the others. Burned and in pain, her victim could do nothing but admit defeat.

How many other miseries had she inflicted upon her? The glasses of urine had she forced her to taste through the sole power of her imagination. The body she rendered bloated; the features she made ugly. The degrading postures she made her hold through nothing but the power of her mind. How many times had she implored her guru, kissing not just the hem of her dress but God knows what else? And the permanent feeling of humiliation and weakness was even more difficult, as she had always looked down upon this sister who put her through so much. She was reduced to obeying someone she saw as being the most banal and the least brilliant of young women. Could there be a worse imprisonment that this?

However, she had always been a little free, in her own way: in her mind. Had people not said she was crazy well before the Problem? She had always refused the *merqouchettes'* ugly and conformist lives; she preferred the lofty, though painful, solitude to the chattering of false friendships. And was she not the one who—when terror reigned—defied all threats and fears by letting her brown hair luxuriate in the sunshine and mock, through its splendor, the wrathful bearded men?

Back then, even the bearded men did not dare challenge her. They knew this silent and unusual neighbor. And they, too, perhaps in spite of themselves, were struck with respect when in the presence of this solitary soul and her impenetrable gaze. That was a long time ago. Now people laughed at her strangeness, at the ideas she spread without saying a word, at her gaze that had become troubled, at her body that often trembled, having been deserted by any sense of tranquillity. Now she earned a daily fill of obscenities and insults. Now she felt miserable and scared. Except during those moments of anger, each one superb and each one majestic.

But what were these small freedoms, these small protests, next to the lives of spies, warriors, and artists, which were so very rich and so very perilous! And Asmahan was all of this. Chahira studied the singer's face. Fascinating! She saw something masculine and determined in the angular contours of this woman's beautiful face. There was also something mysterious in the blue-green eyes that contrasted with her deep dark hair.

Would she have wanted Asmahan's life? Despite the extra weight she now carried, was she not almost as beautiful and was not her voice melodious, though less powerful than the singer's? Obviously, this grotesque question became steadfastly insistent. Could she have been, or would she have wanted to be, Asmahan? To live at the tremendous emotional speed of an artist, a lover, and a spy? To shine, be adulated, and taste every excess and danger before the flower of youth faded, before her exquisite nature was lost?

To die at thirty-two, after having lived with such intensity and ceding nothing: what a beautiful ending Asmahan had! Instead of that, here she was, having misplaced her youth somewhere along the way, piteously knocking on the door of her forties, that stupid and vulgar age which had neither depth nor grace, just like her body, now too heavy, at the mercy of her curves. This age that had neither youth's dreamy pride nor the wisdom of those who had lived for too long.

And yet she would waltz! What kinds of partners were there for this forty-something's massive, rigid, and slightly awkward body? A handsome Austrian of the same age? Klaus, that is what his name would be. Where had she heard that name? Was it in some stupid German police series? It did not matter. He would be Klaus, and that's all . . . Could she really hope for that? She tried to convince herself that she could; her face was magnificent after all! She would work on her clumsiness; she would practice.

Layali el uns fi Vienna
Nasimha min hawal el ganna
Nagham fi lgaww louhranna
Semeeha el tir baka ou ghanna . . .

The beautiful actresses danced, light and smiling. Chahira slowly got up, humming the enchanting lyrics, and started to twirl. Yes, she was the bird, both sad and happy. She slowly closed her eyes and leaned her head against Klaus's shoulder. He was tall; a few white hairs had modestly settled in throughout the light chestnut hair at his temples. His soft blue eyes fell lovingly upon her own face's dark beauty.

A *merqouchette* suddenly started laughing when Chahira's prince whispered sweetly in her ear. The others' laughter followed; she went red with shame and anger. But the dancer's strong arms gently rested on her shoulders, while a "Hush," murmured with infinite tenderness, encouraged her to relax and ignore the jealous ones' snickering.

Her strained features gradually relaxed. She felt light, light; she spun with more enthusiasm, forgetting everything around her, ignoring even Mohand's vexed grunts and Nacer's astonishment, for he knew how to appreciate this type of refinement.

Layali el uns fi Vienna
Nasimha min hawa el ganna . . .

She was off, somewhere else. She did not hear the door burst open.

"My God, grant us your protection! This girl will be the death of me; this girl will be our downfall! There is no worse madness than this, my God, no worse madness!"

Her mother's lamentations ripped her from her daydream.

"You truly have no concept of shame, do you? How old do you think you are? Wake up! You are forty! What have I done to deserve this calamity! My God, what did I do?"

"Stop your moaning, right now. And give us a break!"

"And now you have the gall to speak! Have you no shame! You're forty, don't you get it? Women your age aren't mothers— they are grandmothers! Do you hear me? Grandmothers! And here you are, dreaming away like a child!"

"Leave me alone!"

"We've left you alone for too long! You've only ever done whatever you wanted! You've played the crazy lady for so long that now you really have become one. And I, for one, want nothing to do with a crazy girl. She can only bring us shame."

"You're the crazy one! Get out of my room. Now."

The volcano within her suddenly grumbled to life. She moved in on her mother, hoping to push her out the door. But the mother, also a volcano, grabbed her by the neck and delivered harsh blows to the head.

"It's true. You really are crazy. The only thing left is to take you to the asylum and be rid of you."

The young woman brusquely shoved her away. She wanted to insult her, to shake the woman who had provoked her in this way; but she wound up saying in a rough and sarcastic voice:

"You poor thing. You wouldn't dare! You'd be too afraid of what people would say about you if your daughter was in the asylum. People: you know full well that you live for them!"

"Well, how about that. You must be gifted! That's the only thing you know how to do: talk. You snake. Listen, people or not, I can't put up with you anymore, and I want you out."

"I've heard that one too many times. Why don't you try something else."

But the mother would not be intimidated by her daughter's sardonic stance. She took her by the arm, forcing her to look her in the eye: "I'm telling you, I've had enough of your games. Either you obey my every word or you clear out."

"Obey your every word? In your dreams!"

"Poor fool!"

It was the mother's turn to assume a tone of contempt. She slammed the door on the way out, proud of having overcome the fear with which the "crazy one" filled her.

XIII

The only thing left for her to do was leave. That was what her wounded pride told her every day since that awful fight. Now she had to be the one to slam the door.

These people who did nothing but object to every little thing she did, cast blame on her in every argument, bluntly tell her to be quiet each time she opened her mouth, or insolently ignore her words—for these people she was always and systematically in the wrong—why would she stay with them? Why would she keep putting up with them when they did not respect her forty years, and they laughed at her illness?

She would not let them keep treating her like a crazy woman any longer; they would never again threaten to commit her. Never again. She would leave. Tizi N'Tlelli would welcome her with open arms. Tizi N'Tlelli would grant her a lovely little apartment with rent that would not overwhelm her modest resources. And she would at last savor the joy of having a place of her own that she could run the way she saw fit. It would be clean and calm and sunny; oh, how different it would be from the sad and perpetually dirty place where she currently lived!

"Chahira, women don't live alone in this rotten dump of a country," murmured a voice inside—a shy voice that just barely dared to interrupt her excitement. "And remember that you don't look your age. A young single woman doesn't live alone; don't forget that."

But why, exactly, would a woman not live alone?

To continue at the age of forty to live with your family, who on every God-given day tells you they have had enough of you still living at home. To be subjected to your mother's daily vociferations. Her reproaching you for being clingy. Her telling you what you should and should not do. Her hovering over you as if you were a child. All of this under the pretext of your not being married! Like all single women her age, she might have resigned herself to stoically accept these humiliations, were it not for the Problem, the beatings, the insults, and the threats of being committed. But now she could stay no longer. Now her pride was in revolt, and she blessed her illness—it filled her with a newfound power and stifled her fear. Yes, now she knew. She knew that what was called madness was nothing other than the lofty call of freedom celebrating the "I's" triumph and giving a full-throated laugh at the pitiable conventions that it superbly destroyed.

She had heard that women could live alone in the capital. Ah, the capital! That other planet, where girls went out when they wanted; where some smoked or even got drunk in night clubs and danced until dawn, their bodies pressed against their handsome partners. That might have held some interest, but the truth was that this did not appeal to her in the least. Her somber and dour character had little use for the discotheques' commotion, binge drinking, taunting, and quick and superficial passion. These were not the reasons she wanted to live alone. What she wanted was to be free from the yoke of those who treated her like a child despite the four decades she had lived and to feel in control of her life, responsible, and mistress of her own destiny. And mostly to escape the fights. To stop hearing the petty and venomous words that hurt her ears and soul every day. To bandage her wounds and savor a peace that had long since been stolen.

She did not think she would find this peace in the capital: it was too big, too loud, too stressful. She would move to Tizi N'Tlelli—the city where beautiful and intelligent people discussed culture and freedom, and where the Singer-Hero's proud songs flowed from every street corner. How could she doubt that in this city of all battles and all springs women could live alone without being chastised?

Delighted by the thought of soon becoming a resident of this city, Chahira devoured that vaunted website her fellow countrymen visited for their deals. Purchases, sales, and rentals of every sort: vehicles, furniture, and, of course, real estate. In Tizi, there was no shortage of apartments for rent. She lingered over photos of furnished units: they seemed new, clean, and welcoming. Which one of these beautiful little homes would be hers?

TIZI N'TLELLI

XIV

"And you will be living here alone, Madame? Your husband won't be joining you?"

"I'm not married."

The real estate agent eyed her suspiciously. With her sharp and refined outfit, her nearly makeup-free face, and her brown hair smartly pulled back, she was the very image of a fully "respectable" woman.

"And why would you want to live here alone?"

"And why wouldn't I, sir? We are in Tizi N'Tlelli, aren't we?"

The man standing in front of her was disconcerted by this unexpected response that was flush with naive self-confidence.

"Yes, of course, Madame. But as you know, I'm not the one who decides. I'll ask the owner and then get back with you as soon as possible."

Of course, he never called her back. When she called him a week later, he apologetically mumbled that the owner had decided to rent the apartment to someone else, a married couple with two children.

She went through the same scenario two or three times. People were surprised that she was not married—for she was visibly older than thirty—that she wanted to move in alone, and that she had also come to look on her own.

"Alone, really alone?"

Mohand, Nacer, and a few other young male specters whose names she did not know appeared. Surely she was not alone! And so she wanted to say, ironically, "I can assure you I don't lack for male companionship!" But of course, this was one thing she absolutely could not say. People were not likely to understand what she meant—and that was just as well, for who would want to rent their apartment to a psychotic woman? But the meaning they would certainly have given those few words would have been even more dangerous for her: a woman of little virtue was not worth much more than a crazy woman.

Ultimately, she preferred a lie to self-derision. Of course she was married! But things were not going well with her in-laws; it was better for her to have an apartment of her own. Peace is priceless, right? And my husband? He works in the south. He'll be up once a month.

They did not dare ask her to prove any of this, but suspicion was there all the same.

"We'll be in touch, Madame."

How many times had she heard this false promise? They did call two or three times, each time to tell her that the apartment had gone to someone else.

She started to lose hope. Would she ever have a place of her own? Was she just going to rot away in that forgotten corner of the world called El Moudja? In that prison named the Lahab family? Every night she nervously pored over each new ad on that familiar website. At first, she limited her search to postings that featured pictures; she now resigned herself to looking through those that did not.

Then, one night, for the first time since she started her search, she reached a woman at the other end of the line. She had anticipated this, as the posting said to contact "Samia." Her heartbeat quickened; she instinctively knew that her salvation would come from this voice. Women could also be property owners and rent out real estate: hallelujah!

She wound up with her apartment. At last, a landlord who did not ask for her life story, who did not care whether she was married or divorced. She hardly had to embellish the truth:

"My family decided to move way out by El Moudja. As I work in Tizi now, that really wasn't convenient for me."

"Nothing to worry about. I think you are going to like it here. The previous tenant, she was a civil servant who lived alone with her young boy. There was never the slightest problem; people are laid-back in this city."

Samia agreed to rent the apartment to her for a six-month trial term. Chahira parted with two hundred thousand dinars for rent—a large part of her savings—without the slightest regret. Plus, it was a very reasonable price for a furnished apartment.

XV

A six-hundred-square-meter apartment with two rooms; she could not have hoped for more. Chahira took a tour, her mind elsewhere, thoughts drifting between an atypical past—peaceful in appearance but, oh, how painful—and worrisome questions about the future. What was she going to do with her life now? Win Vienna's Fashion Grand Prix. Well, yes, that would be something! Maybe take some design classes just for that purpose? She would excel, she was sure of it. To be a designer rather than a seamstress, that would be much more . . . prestigious. And, most importantly, to meet someone. To be able to see him. To be able to talk with him about everything and nothing. To be able to smile at him, touch him. To be able to breathe; to be able to live.

She had a sudden desire to join a meet-up site and create a profile where she would say she was rather pretty—at least her face was—but that she was not good at anything apart from drafting sometimes successful patterns for outfits. That she was looking for someone who would let her be the eccentric woman she was and who would not ask her to do the housekeeping, who would nourish her with smiles and tender words, who would place her on a pedestal, and who would not ask for anything in return. Utopian, indeed. No one would respond to such a post.

Her face suddenly grew dark: she had forgotten the worst. In the fresh joy of finally being away from her family, she had forgotten her other prison: the Problem. The ghosts, the shameful smells, the obscene words, the thoughts they stole . . . A teenager had just sworn at her through the wall, much to his friends' delight. Two or three *merqouchettes* burst out laughing as well. Mohand and Nacer grew irritated, less with this crass group than with Chahira, who always involved them in the harassment and arguments she endured.

She decided to laugh about it: go ahead, put all that into the post! "Forty-year-old woman, psychotic—suffering from a range of hallucinations—and hard to live with, seeks a man of the same age, handsome, kind, and stable for a relationship that will last." Oh, that would be a lovely post! It certainly would not lack guts.

But she did not have the courage go through with it. A sudden anguish arose at the very thought of this solitude that she had cherished and closely guarded, which would become a nightmare now that she sought to undo it. What kind of companion could she hope to have now that she was marred by the unspeakable? How could she explain to the "other" that she was, in sum, crazy? Lie? This was a sad situation, where neither truth nor lies could be of much help at all. No matter what she did, she was destined for a life of solitude that, in her new situation, scared her.

So as not to cry or allow despair to kill the new taste of freedom within, she quickly stood up and grabbed a soapy sponge. She, who had only ever been lazy about housework, discovered a burst of unexpected energy. Her new house would be cleaner than the other one—her family's—had ever been. Yes. Her home would be beautiful and happy. So, too, would her life.

XVI

However, this question was a daily torment. The Problem threatened to condemn her to eternal solitude; she had to get rid of it in order to have any hope of a normal life. To have friends, a lover, and who knows, maybe even a family. A family! The very thought of that word surprised her. She, a wife and mother!

A mother? But why? To get a daily dose of crying and cleaning up incontinent orifices leaking human waste? To destroy her youth and health, when so little of either remained, with sleepless nights, endless worrying about an illness, trouble at school, bad friends? Then arrive at the autumn of her life both exhausted and bitter about having done nothing but create ungrateful adults too busy with their own petty dramas to offer a shred of concern for you. So a mother scowls and poisons these selfish children's lives. She lectures her twenty-something daughter because she would rather make herself look pretty or spend time with her friends than she would do housework or cook. She criticizes her clothes, which she deems brazen, and her manners, which she finds to be just as bad: the daughter glares back; she has a loud mouth and an easy laugh. What a disrespectful generation!

Of course, she will be a touch more indulgent with her son's machinations—boys will be boys after all—but she will be surprised to wind up hating him when she finds out about his girlfriend, a sweetheart who will surely possess every variety of shortcoming; who is less attractive than he is and undoubtedly mean as a bee and incredibly manipulative; and who, if she earns the misery of becoming his wife, the mother will endlessly criticize and slander. In short, she will put her through the wringer.

Yes, the mothers she knew were like this. But it seemed that this was not the rule, or that at least it was starting to change. Mothers were becoming more loving, less nervous, less bitter toward younger women. In short, mothers were more fulfilled. Yet she held on to a mistrust of this category of woman. Where had she heard that motherhood was nothing more than a desire for control and, therefore, for power? That was from a long time ago; she did not remember when. Surely something else her old philosophy teacher, Mr. Rouha, had said. Regardless, she thought it made sense.

Thinking about this, she imagined all those brave women who took pride in their children looking at her with a blend of dread and pity. Yes, they would pity this cynical forty-something woman who knew nothing about maternal love, about the happiness of giving birth, about nursing a child, and even about waking up to the nighttime cries and not being able to fall back asleep. About the joy of seeing those first teeth or first steps and hearing those first words. To be there for the child's life and to watch him grow, laugh, cry, fall down, and get back up again. No, truly, a woman who has not experienced this is someone to pity.

But between her and these women who were so sure of themselves, who deserved the most pity? Had they really experienced every joy, or did they just think they had because they were convinced that being a mother was the best thing that could happen to a woman? Had they wanted to be mothers, or had they simply accepted it without question, as people accept everything written, everything inevitable?

And now here she was starting to want a family. But what kind of stability could she give to a child when she had, until only just recently, always mocked that feminine privilege that is motherhood? Would she know how to hold her little cherub in her awkward arms? Would she know how to get through sleepless nights when she so loved her sleep, or the crying when she herself had become so fragile? Given how distracted she was, would she remember to feed him and change his diaper? Would she soon grow weary of him as one does a cumbersome toy? And then, why must she ask herself all these questions, when women got married and had children and managed it all as though nothing could be easier? Yes, she was to be pitied! She was to be pitied and especially to be laughed at for being in her early forties and still asking herself these types of questions. Why was everything with her nothing but endless questioning?

As for questions, there were more pressing ones. How was she going to find work now? Have clients to her home now that she lived alone? No. Even in Tizi N'Tlelli, she would still need to be careful . . . of course, she could join some workshop, but she would lose so many clients! What she needed to do was go back to El Moudja once or twice a week. Yes. That was the only way to keep her clients. *Khalti* Nouara could take orders and measurements and explain to her what needed to be done. Old Nouara was as meticulous as she was kind; everything would be just fine.

XVII

A rat shot across the small courtyard by the stairwell Chahira had just left. Panicked, she covered her mouth, holding her hand firmly over her lips. But she was too late. The hideous beast had leaped inside and padded its way through the maze of her throat and esophagus. She started choking, thinking she might vomit. She leaned over, heaving, head lowered, mouth wide open, hand pressed on her throat as if to chase away the disgusting creature. At that very moment a man tried to get around her, uttering a barely audible "Pardon me." Shamefaced, she rose and furtively glanced at this neighbor. He did not seem to have noticed her frenzy; surely he thought she had been suddenly become sick. She sighed and went off to run her errands. But the rat was still there, clinging to her limbs, crawling over her clothes, then relentlessly returning to her throat, threatening to stay there for the whole day.

A dark mood hung over Tizi's streets. At eleven o'clock, they were dozing in the drab April weather; they were full of hostility toward the hurried pedestrians who startled them in their ugliness, unceremoniously traipsing through their dusty haze. A strong smell of urine filled Chahira's nose, enveloped her body, and grazed her lips. She opened her mouth, trying to make it easier to breathe, but the liquid only worked its way farther in, while the rat, fleeing this undesirable new guest, finally left her.

She walked into a small food shop and asked for salt. She preferred starting with that so she would not forget this indispensable item later on. The shop assistant, a young man in his thirties who concealed his portliness behind a wrinkled shirt and baggy pants that fell only to his ankles, looked her up and down with a malicious stare that darkened the poorly groomed black beard covering his tanned face. His eyes lingered disapprovingly over the young woman's outfit. She was wearing a loosely fitted top in a fairly striking mustard yellow.

"There's no salt," he at last said, finally looking away from her.

Chahira's face went red. "Yes, there is!" She pointed at the salt.

"Yes, but . . ."

Silence.

"Well . . . I don't know how much it costs," spat the bearded man.

She walked out, mortified. In coming to Tizi N'Tlelli, she had hoped to escape filth, ugliness, and the bearded ones. And these were the first things she encountered! The bearded man's laugh—for had he not laughed?—stayed with her as she made her way through the twisting streets that lead to the town's center. He must also have kicked her, as she had a lingering pain in her calf.

She was going to see so many more bearded men in this Tizi, where she thought she would find few if any at all. Old ones who, heads bowed and prayer beads in hand, walked slowly toward the neighborhood mosque. Forty-somethings whose sullen faces pervaded the shops—often, lingerie shops, as legend holds—which sold their products at unreasonably high prices. Fathers dragging behind them a flock of boys and a moving tent—black and shapeless from head to foot—that is supposed to be the wife. Sometimes, there would also be a little girl, often alone among two or three brothers, her young head of six or seven already covered with a tight scarf. At first, Chahira thought they came from somewhere else, just as she did. But there were far too many of them for this to be true; plus, almost all of them spoke the regional language. As for the typical veil—the one nearly all of El Moudja's women wore—well, one saw nothing but that here. Who would have thought there would be just as many scarves in Tizi? At the Lalla Zineb high school twenty years ago, there were none! The girls, stylish if sometimes empty-headed, were always outdoing each other in "trendy" outfits concealed all the while beneath the extra long blouses that the strict monitors required.

She approached the bus stop that led toward Tajditt, the part of the city where former villagers lived, the ones who had left the countryside some three decades ago. Life was good in Tajditt. Housing cooperatives and businesses shot up like mushrooms; prices were much more attractive than those downtown. On summer nights when the heat wave relented and made way for a gentle breeze, lines of women went out for walks or for some shopping at the corner market, while the old women, stylish in their colorful dresses, gathered to loudly discuss everything and nothing and replicate the lovely ambiance of the villages they had left.

Chahira hurried to find a seat in the back, where there was only room for two people, whereas the middle seats could fit three passengers. It was perfect: she would be able to feel at ease without worrying that some seedy neighbor might brush against her.

Until just recently, she had preferred the front seat right next to the van driver—there were a good thirty centimeters separating her from the driver, and nothing could bother her there. Except for the vicious men who thought themselves clever by sitting right behind her and finding ways to get their hands into her beautiful hair. If she made the mistake of protesting, they would swear it was an accident or, better yet, that they had not even touched her, feigning exasperation in turn and accusing her of grandstanding, of being a "girl with problems." Interminable arguments ensued.

No, it was better to take a seat in the rear. In any case, the front seat was taken by some guy who was already in the middle of a conversation with the driver. Two other women—a veiled one in her thirties and an older one dressed in a long skirt and a full tunic—sat in the middle with another gentleman, while a third guy shared the back seat with Chahira.

"Gentlemen, are you comfortably seated?" asked the driver smilingly before setting off. "And you, ladies?"

"Oh, the women," joked the gentleman next to her, "it's best not to ask them. Nothing's ever right with them; they always find something to complain about."

"Because they're too spoiled! Isn't that right, ladies?"

"Oh yes, that's true," added the other man. "Ever since the last amendment to the Family Code; let's not go there. We no longer have the right to open our mouths, my brother. Even if they beat us, we can't do anything!"

Everyone, men and women, found this quip highly amusing; everyone rushed to express their sympathy for the poor oppressed males. Oh yes, the women certainly had too much freedom now, too much power.

The woman of a certain age had a particularly concerned look: "Yes, times have really changed. Today, rare are those girls who were raised well and who know how to maintain a happy home!"

The young woman next to her agreed; then the two started singing praises to the virtuous woman, this endangered species: a real woman should demonstrate patience and discretion. A husband could have his moods, his piques of fatigue or anger. Who, if not his wife, could understand him? Rather than constantly picking a fight, she should know how to listen to him, obey him, and forgive any wayward behavior. Cover for him if he gets a little too tipsy; wipe the slate clean if he happened to beat her. After all, is there anything all that dramatic about a man who occasionally hits his wife? But these days, women cannot put up with anything. Alas, such lost wisdom!

So this was the Tizi that everyone compared—either to shower it with praise or to curse its infidel inhabitants—to Paris? A city where women themselves asserted that virtue was to be beaten without batting an eye?

Chahira burst out, "Excuse me, but I can't just stand by while you say this. In the twenty-first century, you think it's okay for women to be beaten by their husbands! And women are the ones saying this!"

She had started in a Kabyle laced with a thick Moudjaoui accent; but in spite of her intentions, she quickly became confused and found herself babbling in a linguistic blend that bordered on incomprehensible. The gentleman next to her shot her a mocking glance that was almost scornful. She felt her face go red as she continued.

"You weep at the simple thought of a man being beaten, when women have been beaten for centuries without anyone crying foul!"

"It's not the same thing," said the younger woman. "A woman who hits a man is beyond shameful. *Aïb!*"

Everyone started talking at the same time—except for the man sitting next to her—preventing her from getting a word in edgewise.

"Depraved, I tell you," said the man next to the driver, "that's today's woman for you."

Then he remembered the two women he had just insulted in his haste to attack her; he hurried to add: "Of course, I don't mean to generalize. *Hamdoullah,* there still are 'family-minded girls.' I'm just talking about those who don't know their limits. They are meaner than the Devil, and no one has any authority over them. They spend all their time on the road, wandering. Always far from their home; every day in a new city."

A troubled silence set in. This last sentence was a clear attack on the Moudjaoui woman. It was a thinly veiled allusion to her foreign accent: she was always the depraved woman in a new city.

She felt the volcano within begin to rise, but something in the others' tense silence kept it from exploding.

"Stop," she suddenly called in an icy, aloof voice.

She got off without saying a word. She did not want to start her adventure in Tizi with an argument. Tizi, a city named disappointment.

XVIII

O the days' gentle hum! And that sound, more honeyed yet, of Asmahan! "Imta hateeraf," "Ya Habibi taala ilhaani," the astonishing performance of *Ya touyour,* and of course, forever and always, "Layali El Uns." Chahira sang and sang and sang, studying the artist's serious expression. Were the Oriental singer's jade eyes more beautiful than her own chestnut ones? Deeper, more expressive? She glanced away from the videos she devoured on that familiar site, where millions, maybe billions, of users enjoyed music, movies, and TV shows, to linger once more before her mirror. It reflected a face that was a little chubbier, though the pale lips and tired features were just as fine as ever. Was she still beautiful? And if she was, then for how much longer? Then tears came, prickling her chest; only rarely did they reach her eyes.

She would have like to have had Asmahan's life. To intoxicate the world with her powerful yet melodious voice, which lacked nothing, or at least lacked very little, when compared to the Syrian singer's. To be adulated, applauded in packed music halls. To have admirers transfixed with love, who wrote you impassioned letters, and who agonized when they could not be with you. To have, among them, a select few—because they are handsome, strong, and radiant—who whisper the loveliest things in your ear and deftly whisk you away to seventh heaven in a paradise of sensations. Or who spurned the formality of a lover's speech and set off fireworks to celebrate the fiery triumph of the flesh. And then, between two wild nights of love, or maybe at the very moment of corporeal exultation, to keep your mind alert enough to find the smallest piece of information that could serve you, spy that you are. To cut, like a sublime but ruthless Delilah, the hair of every fervent and naive Samson.

"I wasn't a Delilah. I wasn't that type of spy!" The diva's voice was not angry when she corrected her in this Egyptian language in which she usually sang.

"Your voice is delicious. I don't normally like the Egyptian dialect, but you make it sound so pleasant."

"I wasn't a Delilah," repeated Asmahan, vexed all the same. *"I never spied on my lovers. Plus, they weren't lovers; they were my husbands. And those accursed Brits who ended up killing me were never my lovers. Nor the monstrous Germans!"*

Chahira suddenly grew irritated: *"You were adulated, adored. You loved a few in your time. What did it matter if they were Druze like you or British or German, since you were serving your own? Yes, why are you whining about this now? Why don't you want to be a bewitching Delilah?"*

She waited for a response, but the singer's voice had stopped talking to her, and her face, still pouty, faded little by little. She concentrated once more on her songs.

Layali el uns fi Vienna
Nasimha min hawa el ganna . . .

The preceding song, *Ya Habibi taala ilhaani*, had just finished, and YouTube followed it with that famous Viennese waltz, the young Moudjaoui's favorite. Asmahan sang, surrounded by two elegant gentlemen and beautiful smiling couples who flirted before starting a languorous waltz. Chahira did not tire of watching them.

Adi el habaib aal ganbin
Ih elli fadhel aal gaana*

She stood and began dancing when the singer started that verse. Then she raced into the bedroom, returning with her Viennese dress, which she had just finished sewing. She stood before the large mirror in the hall. The *merqouchettes* burst

---

* With a beloved on either side,
Is this not heaven?

out in rude laughter while she admired the purple flounces, the white lace on the sleeves, and the equally white silk lacing that cinched the waist and bust.

She smiled, proud of the work she had accomplished: "Now here is a dress no one would blush at. Not even Empress Sisi!" One of the *merqouchettes* laughed even louder.

"Shut it!" she yelled in her head. "Sisi. That's the movie I should watch tonight. Let's see if it's on YouTube."

Mohand clapped his hands.

"You like this movie, Mohand? I never would have thought!"

Mohand grumbled something. She smiled: "Yes, you are right; the actress certainly is beautiful. Romy something. Wait, I'll check."

She quickly typed "Romy Sisi Empress" into the search bar and found the name she had forgotten.

"Romy Schneider, Mohand. You can watch the movie with me tonight. But right now . . . I want a dance."

The young man protested. He would not dance for anything in the world. Chahira stood up, offended, and went back to dancing on her own. Her face was serious.

Suddenly, she felt a gentle hand on her shoulder. Mohand, one hand in the young woman's hand and the other on her waist, started to dance awkwardly, not daring to meet his partner's eyes. Chahira dared to lean her head on the young man's chest; he grumbled again, annoyed.

Suddenly, he stopped dancing and brought his hand to his nose: a strong smell of sweat and flatulence arose. The young woman backed away, red with shame.

"I'm sorry!" she whispered mentally.

She sat, heavyhearted, and hurried to close YouTube. This shame followed her everywhere; it would be the same in Vienna, with Klaus. She sat frozen on her bed, ready to burst into tears.

"Don't worry," she suddenly heard. Mohand's invisible hand brushed across her forehead. It was one of the rare times he spoke clearly.

"I'm going to sing you my newest song," he added slowly.

"Yes!" she sighed, full of gratitude.

*

Listening to Mohand sing. Occasionally singing along when he was not too grumpy. Arguing with the *merqouchettes,* when, in the evening, they keep you from cuddling up with your new lover. Winding up sleeping in this well-chosen lover's arms after a heroic war against rude and violent bullies.

Sleeping as much as one wanted and waking up at ten in the morning, if not later, to go wander around the dour and anxious city, and returning with arms full of a few purchases: bread, chicken, vegetables, and, most importantly, soda. Making something to eat—once or twice a week, no more. Doing a bit of cleaning, also just once a week. Doing a little sewing and listening to music on YouTube. Listening mostly to Asmahan, while dreaming of a beautiful waltz in Vienna. O the days' gentle hum in Tizi N'Tlelli . . .

XIX

"Tizi truly isn't what it used to be. I may sell this little shop and return to Ighighden, the village where I was born."

"It would be a crime to close such a wonder," said Chahira as her eyes wandered over the tulle dolls hanging from the shop walls. "And what about me, Ammi Amar? Where else would I get such beautiful tulle and lace this white? And who would tell me wonderful stories in this city where I hardly know anyone?"

She did not say this only to be polite. Her gaze lingered upon the old man's small sparkling eyes, his hair and moustache, both of which were completely white, and his slightly hunched frame; she was filled with emotion. Yes, she very much liked this old man, who was so gentle and eloquent. Yes, she would be sad if he deprived her of this place draped in an old-fashioned beauty and his long conversations. And it was a comfort knowing that, in the grey loneliness cloaking her soul, she was still capable of growing attached to someone. For who else did she love apart from this elderly aesthetic and debonair man? Nobody. Except maybe *Khalti* Nouara, who had taught her to sew. And for that, too, she was appreciative: it was the only thing that still bound her to humanity, that kept her from becoming dehumanized.

Amar looked at her with tenderness, as if he had guessed her thoughts—or at least detected the sincerity of what she had said.

"My girl, you still think this is a city? But what part of Tizi N'Tlelli truly remains? You told me yourself that it no longer resembles the place where you'd gone to school. The women and young girls who walk out of Lalla Zineb now are often covered from head to toe. They wear such long hideous scarves and shapeless dresses that they sweep the dusty streets with them. Oh, when I think of my Ouiza's elegance! *Llah Llah!*"

The old man teared up at the thought of his deceased wife. He was quiet for a moment, dreaming. Certainly he was thinking about this woman who was young and beautiful just a few decades ago. Chahira knew this because on many occasions her friend had shown her an aging black-and-white photograph of Ouiza. She must have been a bit younger than thirty. Shapely, she wore a close-fitting tunic and a flared skirt that fell just below her knees. Her rich brown hair was pulled into a bun; a few curls escaped. She was laughing, head tilted back, revealing a slender neck and nice teeth.

"Yes, she was beautiful," she said at last.

"Beautiful and forever young. Even when she died, she died among the young. The young who were drunk on idealism and freedom."

The widower said these last words in French—a French that many men of his generation spoke. A refined French but with rolled r's and a light, lilting accent. The young woman loved listening to this language which was at once refined and hybrid. She let him tell her, for the nth time, about the sad demise of this joyous woman, who lost her life to a stray bullet during the Hijacked Spring demonstrations. He told Chahira about how she died with a smile on her lips; how hundreds of Tizeans had attended her burial; how their only son, who lived in France, could not attend; and how this absence had caused a deep rift between them. He also told her about how he had cried tears of love for her and how he saw her in a dream three years later: she reproached him for having cut ties with his son and asked him to reconcile.

"And do you know what Meziane told me?"

Chahira knew. Amar had already told her that his son had also seen his mother in a dream and that she had begged him to seek his father's forgiveness. Of course, Chahira did not say a word. She let her friend finish his story. Then the two of them were silent for a long moment before Amar slowly continued with a sigh.

"But even that awful time—one full of bullets and tear gas, one that took my dear wife's life—was better than what we have now."

The young woman looked at him with astonishment.

"There was still life in this town, my girl, and still hope. People—especially young people—had hoped to change things. They fought, they resisted; they dreamed of a better life. They had ideals. Can we say the same thing today?"

Chahira thought about the idle youths she saw every day at the bottom of her building when she came home. They stood in the stairwell, headphones on, mechanically humming songs with banal lyrics devoid of poetry, but Chahira sometimes found the songs funny and lighthearted, like the one that then came to mind:

Ya loumima ghir dei liya
Ndjibha anoucha poupiya
Felbidha rani nsuivi
Khelouni hakem le Wifi
Dayerha amour*

Watching the young girls in the distance, they played cards or dominos or loudly shared private jokes. But at night, they exchanged other things. Chahira was fully aware that her neighborhood teemed with dealers and users. Sometimes their secret transactions went awry and violent fights ensued. You could hear the screams, insults, and, on rare occasion, profanities.

Then she thought about the others, slightly younger ones, who haunted the mosques in her neighborhoods in Tizi and in El Moudja. They went five times a day, posture rigid, and gaze fervent. They also dealt in transactions. They bought or sold Qurans, books to interpret the word of God and his Prophet's hadiths, prayer beads, incense, candles, kohl, and henna. Some people said that, for this group, the white powder that opened Paradise's doors was standard currency. Did they have ideals? Maybe yes, as opposed to those with the gel-plastered hair and

---

* Pray, my dear mother,
That I marry a Barbie doll
Me, I follow the light-skinned girl's feed
Chill, I connect to the Wifi—
In "love" mode.
(Cheb Houssem, "Choufibentekmadaretfiya" [2017])

sagging pants who thought of nothing but the latest fashion trends and chasing after girls. Girls who, just barely beyond childhood, had every beauty secret at their fingertips—or rather at the tips of their fingernails, which were always impeccably done; their looks just as meticulous as the painstakingly applied makeup on their faces. Once they reached the age of fifteen or sixteen, no trace of innocence remained on those adult faces, full as they were of deceit and cunning—the only forms of intelligence that were still in style. Only just teens, they were already women; and they dated many, not because they were of an age when the body, discovering new sensations that were as troubling as they were exquisite, sought exultation, but because they were already in search of a husband, one who was as rich as possible.

Well, perhaps unlike them, the mosque rats did have ideals. But morbid and dangerous ideals they would be better without . . .

She was pulled from her thoughts by her ghosts' groaning— Mohand leading the charge. "You know I can't stand those bearded ones," he seemed to say. "They hate the musician that I am . . ."

"People today, the young, they won't fight," Ammi Amar continued, "they have no ideals. At the very least, they could fight for the right to wear a Kabyle dress or to eat dried figs"— and then he burst out in teasing laughter. "Well, of course, one shouldn't try for too much! And then they get all bogged down by tradition. Folklore. And never find their way back out again."

A *merqouchette* laughed; Mohand too. Chahira also started laughing. Now here was a man who knew how to wield irony. And there was something incongruous, funny even, about the way this almost toothless mouth put tradition on trial. Yes, in El Moudja as in Tizi—wherever you went in this accursed country, for that matter—everyone only ever swore by tradition. A lethal tradition. She was glad he felt the same way she did; she restrained herself from applauding.

Yet it was not true that people had stopped protesting in Tizi N'Tlelli. She had heard that the MITN—the Movement for an Independent Tizi N'Tlelli—was growing in numbers; that more and more men and women were secretly joining. Yes, it seemed that many Tizeans dreamed of having their own country. And how awful was that! What would become of people like her if that happened? Would she need a passport—maybe even a visa—to be in this city she loved in spite of everything?

"And the MITN, Dda Amar," she timidly asked. "What do you think about the MITN?"

The old man startled—or at least that was what the forty-year-old woman thought. She could no longer trust her senses, and she had had her doubts a few times when it came to this friend for whom her admiration held no limits.

He stammered, "I'd prefer not to talk about that. All I can say is that nothing exists without good reason. Especially when it keeps growing in size . . ."

He suddenly fell quiet. Two hulking men had just entered the shop. They were also in their forties and wore slightly faded jeans, brown V-neck sweaters, and black leather jackets, or maybe it was fake leather. From a distance, they looked like twins. But they did not look all that much alike. One had brown skin, a mustache, and thick black hair; the other had no mustache and curly light brown hair. They surveyed the store as if looking for something; then the darker one quickly asked if they had wool. "Blue wool," he added flatly after a few seconds. He spoke in a perfect Kabyle.

"*D lxir kan*,"* Amar responded. And then they left.

Were her senses playing a trick on her? Chahira thought she saw fear in her friend's eyes.

---

* The literal meaning of this phrase is "[we have] only what is good." This Kabyle expression is used to indicate that a person does not have what was requested of them.

XX

The latest visit to El Moudja had gone poorly. *Khalti* Nouara had, however, been happy to see her. Just as her former protégée had requested, she had put out an ad explaining that Madame Lahab had temporarily changed addresses but that her clients could continue to leave their orders with the older woman. That was enough to keep the orders flowing in as before. Nouara graciously took the measurements and noted all other important details in her precise schoolgirl handwriting, which she had carefully maintained since childhood. A childhood spent in the capital, in a poor neighborhood where she was one of the few daughters sent by their fathers to gain a bit of education in the *roumis*' elementary schools.[*]

She was methodical about keeping everything in an old notebook she showed Chahira during each weekly visit. The good woman then offered her a tea or coffee, which she served with *khfaf*, those traditional and ever so delicious beignets—which goes to show that tradition was not all bad—that she continued to make with her wrinkled and slightly trembling hands that were just as skilled as ever.

"Do you like where you're living, my girl?" she asked softly.

"Yes, *Khalti* Nouara. You're thoughtful to be concerned."

"You're like a daughter to me, Chahira. That's why I permit myself to give you advice. Listen to me, and please don't get upset."

"I know what you're going to say, *Khalti*. You told me last week and the week before that."

"Yes, and I'm going to say it again, because I'm worried about you. I know you are a 'quiet' young woman who doesn't

---

[*] In Algerian dialect, the word *roumi* signifies, in a very general sense, "French" or "European."

just go and get carried away by any old thing, as most girls to-day tend to do. But a well-raised girl, however serious she may be, doesn't live alone, my dear. People are not angels, and what is more, they are fast talkers . . ."

"*Khalti,* I know you mean well, but I'm forty, and . . ."

"What is forty? I'm thirty years older and sometimes I feel I've so much more to learn from life! And your own forty years in particular . . . What I want to say," added Nouara, her voice full of kindness, "is that you are treasure of a woman, but you have to recognize that you get all fired up over nothing and sometimes you forget to keep your head on your shoulders."

"Come on, *Khalti,*" Chahira answered, smiling indulgently in turn. "Proof: I didn't get fired up over that."

"That's because you have a special respect for me. I know this." The old woman's smile grew as gentle as ever.

"Absolutely. And as you know, you never stop taking advantage of it, *Khalti!*"

"Well, as I should!"

And the two women started laughing. No, of course she was not mad at the old woman. How could she be angry with this wellspring of sweetness? Sweetness—that rare quality she had never seen in that woman who was not as old but who was so much more ill-tempered: her mother, Rabéa.

"So you just now remembered that you have a mother and a family?" Rabéa happened to say. "I know you visited Nouara two weekends in a row and that you don't stop over here . . ."

"*Yemma,* given how you treated me the last time, you can't be surprised that I don't want to set foot in here . . ."*

"Perhaps you wanted me to greet you with ululation? Count yourself lucky that we even answered the door! The only reason I did is because people here still don't know why you've left for good."

"Great, well, since I'm bothering you, I won't stay. Just let me grab a few papers."

"Papers? To do what?"

"I'm going to register for some classes. For a fashion design program."

* *Yemma* means "mother" in Arabic and Kabyle.—*Trans.*

"A program in what? You think you can go to school at your age? When will you understand that you aren't young anymore, that you're almost old? You should be thinking of starting a family before it is entirely too late . . ."

The visitor tried her best to stay calm: "*Yemma,* this is exactly why I left: to not have to listen to your endless criticism anymore . . ."

"No," shouted the mother, "you left because you're brainless; you've always been that way!"

"I'm leaving. I didn't come to be insulted."

The mother shrugged her shoulders and responded derisively: "Yes, if you can't stand hearing the truth, leave. You have always been brainless and worthless."

Chahira slammed the door on her way out, shaking with anger. She thought she saw the neighbor woman across the way startle from behind her ox-eye window.

XXI

"Lahab!"

"Lahab!"

"Lahab-Lahab!"

"Laa-haab!"

Ever since she got back from El Moudja, ever since her latest fight with her mother, her whole neighborhood buzzed with these two syllables. They passed through walls, windows, and furniture. Dozens of masculine voices, grave or quaking, friendly or threatening, serious or amused—often amused— rang out from everywhere, repeating her last name. A name she had never told anyone. How had her neighbors discovered it? Who knew her in this accursed neighborhood?

Chahira had hoped to get a little rest in bed, but she quickly got up and glanced out the window with worry. She had imagined young people gathered below her window, waiting for her to appear and surreptitiously repeating "Lahab." Everything seemed deserted, however; she did not see anyone outside. She closed the window, not knowing what to think.

"Lahab!" yelled a jeering voice as soon as she turned her back.

It came from by the window. She held her breath for a few seconds and then decided to relax and ignore what she had heard.

"Lahab!" someone snickered from the other side of the room.

Other voices followed, shooting out from all around. The young woman crouched in the corner of the living room, head in her hands. She rocked in distress, back and forth, moaning softly. The hideous, teasing voices that yelled her name did not stop. Chahira suddenly went rigid. An invisible hand had just grabbed her breast and then advanced between her legs. From all around, other hands toyed with her body, while the voices continued to contemptuously say her name. She stretched out her arms to shield her body, trying to protect herself from these ghostly attackers. But nothing stopped; she then succumbed to the ultimate breach, one that, like an *assegai,* attacked her femininity.* She stood, leaning against the wall, out of breath, covered in sweat.

She thought about seeking refuge outside. Was it not said that contact with the Real, with others, chases demons away? Plus, it would do her some good to get out and walk in the almost-empty streets. She dressed quickly and went out.

It was fine at first. It calmed her to be walking alone on this first of May, spurned by passersby . . . Well, not entirely: three young men leaned against a crumbling, darkened wall. A chill ran through Chahira; this happened every time she walked by a group of young people or children.

"Lahab!" an impudent voice called.

She stopped and stared at the three idle men. She was sure the one in the middle, the tallest, had called her name. The volcano within erupted.

"Is there a problem? Are you talking to me?" Her face burned with anger.

"*Wech omri?*† Can't get enough of me? Come here, beautiful . . ."

She furiously spat on the ground and stalked off, leaving a wake of curse words behind. The three punks snickered.

She wandered for another half hour, cheeks red with shame and anger, tears slowly spilling from her tired eyes. Then she returned home, spent and bruised. The voices seemed to have stopped.

But at night, the ghosts won. And on that specific night, Chahira found no respite. Just as a few hours earlier, before she had gone on her walk, hundreds of hands violated her body, brazen laughter assailed her, and her name kept coming from below her apartment. What could be more terrifying for a young woman than hearing her name yelled by malicious males outside her home?

---

* In this context, an *assegai* is a type of spear common to southern Africa.—*Trans.*

† "What's wrong, sweetheart?"

She suddenly sat up in bed. There was someone knocking softly at her door. Knocking at her door? Was someone really calling her name? She didn't know; she no longer knew anything. She put her head back in her hands and slowly rocked back and forth, back and forth. And while in this little trance, verses came to mind, superb and uncontrollable. She recited aloud:

العالم كله يهلل باسمي، ينادي به صباحا مساء
العالم كله يهلل باسمي، ينادي به صباحا مساء
و أنا كتمثال بوذا، جالس القرفصاء
فلم أبالي ولم أتولى، أ فليس إلى الأنبياء يساء؟
فإن اكفهر وجهي ارتدوا جميعا، وصمتوا كلهم، رجالا نساء
وقالوا يا أخت، ما أنت فاعلة؟ فأقول اذهبوا، أنتم التعساء*

And all at once, the voices were gone. No more invisible hands. Silence; peace. Rest! Rest at long last! The young woman tried to repeat the redemptive poem. From the midst of a million demons, an angel had whispered to her the words of victory, of invincibility. Then she ran to her computer. She had to write down these magical words.

Yes, it could only have been an angel who uttered them: an angel sent by God. For it had been so long since she had penned any lines! She had stopped writing them a year or two after leaving Lalla Zineb. Plus, she did not remember ever being able to write poems in Arabic. Her poems in high school—the ones that often came to her mind—were all written in French. It is true that her world had become Arabized since leaving Tizi, because people only loved Arabic in El Moudja. Like all the girls in her region, she had started watching Egyptian or Syrian soap

* The whole world glorifies my name, repeating it morning and night.
The whole world glorifies my name, repeating it morning and night.
I remain unshakeable, like a Buddha in the lotus position:
Why worry? Why look away? Have we not always lashed out at the prophets?
All it takes is for my face to darken for all men and women to abandon their convictions and fall silent.
Then they ask me, "Sister, what will you do with us?" And I answer, "Leave, you wretches!"

operas, or Mexican ones dubbed in Arabic. French had been cast into an oubliette. She watched the news in Arabic. Read in Arabic. But she had never written poems.

A chill passed through her. But it was not a poem! Of course not! She was correct in thinking an angel had sent her these rhymes. And what if this was the reason for her illness? A test from God that concluded with the revelation of her sainthood? Yes, she was certainly chosen by God! A saint, or maybe a prophetess . . .

A *merqouchette* laughed, pulling her from her thoughts. "Lahaab!" she yelled maliciously, laughing all the while.

That was the first time a female voice said her name.

"Lahab, Lahab!" other voices called.

XXII

What to do? What to do? Day and night they knocked on the door and ran off. Night and day, they quietly jeered, "Lahab, Lahab." And of course, night and day, libidinous specters groped her, violating her body and mind, while female onlookers, who were just as spectral, howled with laugher. Stomach gripped with panic, insults on her lips, legs trembling, she saw her sanity slip away, swiftly slip away. This was insanity, the real kind, the dark kind this time. The one where the Real disappeared, lost between threatening harpies, gruesome laughter, and orgiastic dances. The one that, if it swallowed you, would leave you no chance of returning to the light.

What to do? Go back on medication? Make official her affiliation with the kingdom of the insane? What a bitter defeat! She had been on medication for a while when she was still in El Moudja. She remembered what it had done to her. She remembered the black tunnel that had devoured her, the zombie she had become, the way she lost track of her things and was incapable of working. How would she get through this now that she lived alone? No. Going back on olanzapine was out of the question. She, so detestably proud, could not resign herself to seeking help. People never respected or felt any compassion for those who bartered away their pride; and when she imagined herself bowing before this medication, she envisioned it taking a cutting delight in reducing her to human rags and laughing all the while at her degradation . . .

But what could be done? How could she get to the other side of the Problem without abdicating, without giving in to psychiatry's diktat? This accursed psychosis, where did it come from, what was its origin? Maybe by going after the source . . . Yes, of course! A psychologist rather than a psychiatrist! She had to try. It is true that Chahira had no love for this race of

Freudian creatures; she did not trust them. To her, they were nothing but a bunch of voyeurs who doubled as greedy charlatans. How else could they be described, these individuals who savored their patients' tragic or salacious pasts and who, after satisfying their unhealthy curiosity, pocketed an astronomical sum while mentally rubbing their scheming hands together? Yes, those were psychologists for you. But she had to try something. Maybe she was wrong about them. Maybe they were a big help to the poor despairing creatures who met with them; and maybe the money they earned was next to nothing considering the services they provided. Yes, maybe the key to all her sorrows could be found. Unearth her past, which looked so calm on the surface but was so turbulent; confront it; wage war against it to finally reconcile with it. To finally move on.

Oh, she had plenty stored up for the shrink's "therapeutic" curiosity. She could tell him about the childhood nocturnal fear that gripped her very the moment she went to bed—the window by her bed had overlooked a cemetery. She had imagined the dead leaving their tombs to get into bed with her; she had expected to see them wandering around her bedroom uttering the typical comic strip "boos." She had started to count in her head to fall asleep quickly and put them out of her mind, but this always took much longer than she would have liked. And before she fell asleep, the timid thought of talking with her mother about it, to ask her to move her bed, came to mind. But she always abandoned the idea as soon as she awoke: she would not put herself in a position to be treated like a coward or ridiculed. The six-year-old girl's pride vehemently rejected this possibility.

She could also bring up a fight she had had with a classmate when she was in her second year of elementary school. Her name was Hayet and she was a real pain; and Chahira had the great misfortune of one day asking her to return a coloring book she had loaned her. The "pain" refused to return it and challenged Chahira to a duel, so to speak. "We'll fight at 3:30, outside the school, right when class ends." Lahab was a slight and peaceable child, and she was a bit afraid of this confrontation. But she did not run away. When the bell rang,

Fatma-Zohra, her tablemate, whispered in her ear, "Right when the fight starts, bite her so hard that she'll never be able to forget it." Words that warmed her heart. Fatma-Zohra was a good girl. But Chahira was not very aggressive, and her adversary came out on top. She returned home, hands bleeding, and had to tell her incredulous mother that she had fallen on some broken glass. Rabéa tried to learn the truth, but her daughter told her nothing about the fight. Many years later—when she was more than thirty—her mother told her that Hayet Leghoud had died following a brief illness. Excellent news, of course; served that cow right! She was overcome with joy.

She especially wanted to talk with the shrink about that hand that maliciously grazed her left nipple each time she went to the corner grocery. About her burning face, about the tears, about the dread that tortured her each time her family sent her to the store to buy milk or a jar of jam. She had never said a word about this to her mother, just as she had never talked with her about that stranger who had violently slapped her on her way to school, right before he stuck his finger inside her most private of parts. She was not yet ten. She had returned despondent, eyes dead, head down, and shut herself in the bedroom she still shared with her sister, who had since married. She did not take a shower, as it seemed women typically did when their bodies had been violated. She did get a little food down. But she walled herself off behind such an eloquent silence that even her mother grew deeply concerned about her. Rabéa begged her to tell her what was wrong, to trust her. But she simply did not trust her. In any case, what could this mother do apart from lamenting and beating her chest or face and telling her not to say a word to anyone? Of course, she might have whispered a word or two of consolation, or many, or even—O miracle—caressed her cheek or hair. But what was more likely was that she would throw this sad incident back in her face, scolding her for being the type of idiot that everyone chooses to fondle. She would scream at her, as she always did, and then everyone would hear what had happened. And everyone would laugh.

Yes, she could tell all that to a psychologist.

*

Madame N. never smiled—or almost never. She asked well-prepared questions in her quiet voice that was monotone and neutral; she methodically noted the responses in a notebook. How old are you? What do you do for work? Are you married? Are your parents still alive? Are you the oldest, middle, or youngest child?

Chahira answered the questions just as mechanically as they were asked. Already she hated Madame N. She hated her small brown eyes that ended in crow's feet, her expressionless eyes, her round glasses that were as outdated as her bun—which would have been more fitting for last century's elementary schoolteachers—and most of all, the phlegmatic and impersonal tone with which she spoke to her, and, undoubtedly, to the rest of her patient-clients. In a few minutes, she would stop with the questions and then it would be Chahira's turn to talk and talk and talk.

Of course, the shrink asked about her childhood. She suddenly remembered that movie with Robin Williams she had seen a few years before—it was called *Will something;* she could no longer remember.* It was about a teenage boy, gifted in mathematics, whose delinquent behavior gave his teachers a run for their money, and the same was especially true for all the psychologists he was made to see. He knew their worthless theories and prepackaged explanations by heart. He refused to talk about himself, preferring to invent memories of experiences and reactions he had not had. He made psychologists believe he was under hypnosis when he was not; that he was cooperating when he was simply jerking them around. And what if she did the same thing? What if she invented things to tell Madame N.?

No, that would not make any sense! Had she not come of her own free will to try to put an end to the Problem? She had to try. Give herself over, bare herself. She started, hesitant, to talk about the solitary and absentminded little girl that she was; about her mother who never got over bringing her into the world and who only ever heaped complaints and insults upon her; about her

---

* The film being remembered is *Good Will Hunting* (1997).—*Trans.*

impassive father who was often indifferent to everything. She stopped suddenly, not knowing whether she should talk about the episodes she had promised herself she would tell. Not really knowing whether she could go through with it.

"Have you ever experienced any trauma?"

Chahira fell silent, nervously twiddling her fingers. Was she really going to share her most painful and shameful secrets with this woman whom she did not know and who seemed cold and unpleasant? The shrink looked at her for the first time and gave a smile of encouragement.

"Beatings, violence, sexual assault, for example?"

And it started all over again. Madame N. had clearly read her thoughts, as so many others had done before. She must have thought her truly stupid to leave her most private thoughts out in the open like that, within everyone's reach. Yes, she evidently had nothing but contempt for her; plus, the rictus she was trying to pass off as an affable smile betrayed her. And now, she was laughing. On the inside, of course, but she did not know that Chahira could also read her mind. She heard a jeering laugh, like the *merqouchettes'*, but it was clearly the accursed psychologist's voice.

The patient's face went red with anger and shame. It was her own fault; she had come here of her own free will to humiliate herself before this greedy and indifferent woman who was laughing at her. She burst out, "You think this is funny? To violate people's privacy like this? To disrespect them?"

"I did not mean any disrespect," the other softly replied. "Calm down; I must have touched on a sensitive area. Please forgive me; I should not have rushed you."

"Yes, but you were disrespectful. You're talking to me like I'm a child. And you don't need to concern yourself with my private life. Did I ask you to tell me about your family or your darkest secrets?"

"Madame, I don't believe you are ready to talk yet. This is normal. With time, you will learn to trust me. We will end this first meeting now. Things will go better the next time, you'll see."

"There won't be a next time."

She stood up, threw two thousand dinars on the table, and slammed the door behind her.

XXIII

Ammi Amar died. Dragonfly, his beautiful and very refined boutique, was vandalized. By young punks with slurred and incoherent speech and dilated pupils. Yes, druggies, just barely beyond their adolescence. They made fun of the old man's weary and slightly bent body and his bald head. They manhandled his lace and his lovely and delicately embroidered doilies; they made fun of the small tulle ballerinas, precious souvenirs of his dear Ouiza. They threw them on the ground, crushing them while emitting short, slow, quaking laughs. The Aesthete had tried to stand up to them. He told them that he did not have anything in his boutique that they would find useful, that they should go, that he was going to call the police. But their laughter grew more persistent and more menacing.

So he threatened them with his cane, which he sometimes used for walking. He did not want to beat them up; he just wanted to frighten them so they would leave. But when they saw him raise the long wooden stick, they were filled a new and unexpected excitation. They started uttering in unison long lugubrious cries, like a pack of wolves. Two of them began frenetically clapping their hands just two inches from the old man's face. Then one of them grew emboldened and took the glasses from his face. And so, of course, Amar lost his patience. "Take that, you lowlife," he yelled in his tired voice, landing a violent swing of his stick on the guilty one. His friends hooted even louder, and then everything went so fast. The poor Aesthete was insulted, shaken, mistreated, brought down with kicks and swings from his own stick—which they had taken from him— and then left for dead.

Then they quietly took off, they who had been anything but quiet in this store they had sacked, screaming and laughing all the while. They said that, as beaten as he was, Ammi Amar forced himself to gather his little tulle figurines as soon as his attackers left; that he wept as he tried to repair and clean them. But in vain. The poor dismembered ballerinas were covered in dust and his own blood.

But Chahira did not understand. If Amar was alone in the boutique with these barbarians, who could have known what had happened? Had there been witnesses who saw the attack and did nothing to rescue the victim? Or was this another scenario created by Tizeans with fertile imaginations? Because this country did not lack for imagination. Everyone wanted to tell stories, each one more sensational than the last. Everyone was always in the know about everything, without anyone ever seeing a thing. There was always a brother, a friend, or a neighbor who had seen it all. Wasn't this an excellent way to wash one's hands of what had happened? To preserve one's innocence while knowing all? Yes, in this country, everyone knows, but everyone *khatih.*[*]

This happened to be true for more than minor news items. Everyone knew who the country's real leaders, real assassins, and fake militants were. Of course, there were legions of fake militants; that, too, everyone knew. Pretty much everywhere people whispered about which supposed combatant had never gone off to war, which part of the opposition was really in the pockets of those in power, which others were Western pawns. Yes, people here were full of convictions. When it came to expressing them in person, that was another story. The eternal struggle between Truth and Fear.

Why did Chahira never know anything? Why was she unable to pick out fake combatants, fake patriots, or those feigning virtue in a country where everything was, for that matter, fake? She often wondered where people got their information; it never seemed to reach her, being the poor autistic woman she was.

That night she had hoped that Ammi Amar would know how to get her to forget the Problem, her worsening symptoms, and the humiliation she had felt at the psychologist's. Of course, she would not have told him anything about that. But the stories she had already heard so many times would have

---

[*] Everyone *khatih*: everyone "washes their hands of it."

made her forget her troubles, and her friend's gentle and serene voice would have filled her with a healing affection that chased away anger and resentment. He would mention his Ouiza, whom he cherished despite the long time that had passed; she would admire his tulle dolls and be reminded that beauty still existed and that her proud heart was right to never lose hope for tenderness.

But, of course, from Ammi Amar there was none. Ammi Amar had betrayed her, and not just because he had left her alone—more alone than she had ever been before. Amar was fake; he was like everyone else in this rotten country. Amar, fake! Unbelievable! Maybe Warda was talking nonsense? Just like everyone else, maybe she shared ideas about things for which she had no proof?

Now that Dragonfly was closed, now that the Aesthete was not there for her, the only thing left for her to do was go to Warda's. She did not want to go back to her lonely apartment; there were too many ghosts, and they had become too ruthless. Though they were not overly strong: there was no need for friendships as vast and deep as the ocean to chase away the unwelcome and insolent shadows. The shadows could be drowned in a few drops of spit shaped into conventional sentences, more or less friendly, and then swallowed with a nice hot cup of tea and a few cookies. That summarized her friendship with Warda. She had known her since the beautiful redhead was six. Chahira, who was ten years older, shared the same classroom desk with her older sister Malika—they also shared the same boredom and hatred of the lugubrious place that was Lalla Zineb high school. So sometimes, when the boarding-school teachers freed the boarders on Monday afternoons, Malika invited her classmate from El Moudja to spend the afternoon at her home.

It was anyone's guess as to why the younger sister, the ravishing Warda, became so enamored of this rather taciturn guest who ultimately returned those feelings. She delved into her meager pocket money to buy her treats or small gifts; she invented games that would entertain her protégée. While the young redhead lost none of her beauty as she grew, the fondness she inspired in the one who, in the meantime, became a seamstress diminished considerably. Though as a child she was cheerful and mischievous, she became a conventional and slightly deceitful young woman. Chahira only continued to visit her because Malika, who had moved to the eastern part of the country with her husband a few years before, had designated her to be her sister's personal seamstress after a fashion; she had already made a good part of her trousseau.

A semblance of friendship had grown between the two young women. But there was never any outpouring of feeling, never any request for support or even acts of affection. Only friendly and fairly banal exchanges they shared on the rare occasions when they saw one another. And the tea and petits fours they always served with the same courtesy.

The tea and petits fours were somewhat bitter that day. Not just because Ammi Amar was dead, no, but because what she had just learned about him was too painful. Unsurprisingly, Warda was convinced of what she said: the young men who had beaten the old man were not typical punks. Well, actually, they were notorious punks, of course, but their aggression was far from being gratuitous. "Everyone knows who they roll with," she added with a wink.

There it was again, "everyone knows," except for Chahira. Would Warda be kind enough to explain it to her?

"Well, those who run everything!" she lowered her voice.

Chahira did not want to believe this nonsense. Why would "those who run everything" go after an old guy like Amar the Aesthete? Oh yes, surely those doilies, his lace, and those figurines constituted a serious threat to state security!

But she swallowed that last bit: too much irony for the relatively formal relationship she had with her hostess. The first sentence would be enough.

"You clearly are not from Tizi N'Tlelli, my dear friend!"

And Chahira thought to herself, *It's crazy the ease with which people have used that word over the past couple of years. All it takes is a request to be added on social media for the person in question to drop all formality and call you "sweetie" or "my dear" and send you hearts and kisses and God knows what other oddities from the virtual world. From the first conversation on, and without them ever seeing you.*

"You can tell you're not from here," the hostess insisted. "All Tizeans know that Amar Dragonfly is one of the MITN's dedicated militants!"

Chahira felt her anger rise. This joke was truly in poor taste—just like the nickname "Amar Dragonfly"; the redhead made it even uglier by pronouncing it "Dragonflah." How could one so insultingly defame an old man who had just lost his life, and in such dramatic circumstances? Warda's features suddenly turned hideous, becoming those of a malicious shrew. As she laughed, this shrew was visibly pleased to have shocked her guest.

"His MITN friends often gathered in his boutique. They thought Tizi N'Tlelli had nothing to do with the rest of the country, that contact with the other regions sullied it, making it withdraw and decline into obscurantism . . ."

The woman from El Moudja felt her hostess's nonchalant words like a murderous bullet. Just like, she suddenly thought, one of the bullets that had stolen the lives of those 130 young Kabyles seventeen springs ago. Like her, those who pulled the triggers were foreign to the region; like her, they did not speak the language. She felt a lump in her throat: did Ammi Amar secretly associate her with those executioners who made him a widower? Oh, not intentionally for once; but his Ouiza was good and dead. At their hands.

She saw the dismal faces of El Moudja's men and women. The former's dusty djellabas and the latter's long *djilbabs* sweeping the ground. The bushy beards and the veils that were worn in the manner of Sisyphus carrying the rock on his back. The macabre brown marks the men had on their foreheads to prove that they fervently prostrated themselves while adoring God—an unjust God, since he deprived women, who prayed to him just as much, of these ostensible marks of devotion. No, the women did not have "aureoles" on their foreheads; just early wrinkles and foreheads etched with lines from years of submission and suffering in silence.

Yes, that was El Moudja—and undoubtedly the majority of the country's regions. Even in the capital, women were pale, tired, and often neglected. And the men? Oh, a man in this country is nothing but vain, but without grace, without elegance, and also often without scruples. A man, she thought, is at best a ridiculous creature; at worst, a monstrous creature, and sometimes he is both at once.

In any case, that had to be how Ammi Amar saw El Moudja. Yes, he undoubtedly held her little village in contempt; maybe he held her in contempt as well. A voice within repeated that he was right. In Tizi N'Tlelli, the old women wore vibrantly colored dresses that seemed to laugh in the face of life's difficulties; the young girls went to the university in casual outfits that made them look so pretty and that no one batted an eye at. Like everywhere else in the world, they discussed the previous day's soap opera. Sometimes they complained about their instructors' strictness or about their mothers' or boyfriends' lack of understanding. In El Moudja, too, the girls sometimes talked about those things—life's matters. But those girls from Tizi had a livelier and more joyous air about them.

When they wanted to—even though it was rare—they could also discuss books. They liked to share their thoughts about books in Tizi N'Tlelli. Even if the person was not well educated, even if their sentences were rife with errors, people liked showing that they had devoured Pierre Daco's books and that they knew a bit of Nietzsche and Marx.* Of course, this was especially true with the young men, who liked to claim an allegiance to these great thinkers from whom they often only remembered two quotes: "God is dead" and "Religion is the opiate of the masses," respectively. Chahira had sometimes understood parts of their conversations. She had been shocked by their deplorable French but charmed by their enthusiasm and their dream of remaking the world. Young people never talked like that in El Moudja. So, was Amar the Aesthete right? Did Tizi have to be protected from the nefarious influence of those who wanted to erase from it every trace of beauty, gaiety, and openness?

But then would that affable smile with which he welcomed her and those gentle words he shared with her not be anything more than hypocrisy? He never stopped telling her that she was welcome—but had he actually been dreaming of chasing her away forever? Of forcing her to use a passport each time she

* Pierre Daco (1936–92) was a Belgian psychoanalyst.—*Trans.*

wanted to enter his region—the one he wanted to turn into a country?

A passport, maybe even a visa, to go to Tizi: what a horrific idea! But to say that Amar, that old aesthete she had so loved, was a hypocrite, a liar—that hurt even worse. The one whom she saw as a wise and loving uncle saw her as nothing but a foreigner who had come to pollute his people's minds and threaten their tranquillity! And yet she too loved seeing those beautiful heads of brown hair waving in a soft breeze and listening to young people cite Nietzsche and Marx in their striking accent. She was also full of admiration for the Singer-Hero, treacherously murdered, whose songs she only vaguely understood. And there had to be other "Arabs" throughout the country who shared her tastes and way of thinking. So why?

But, she countered, the Aesthete could not be right. Tizi N'Tlelli was far being a paradise. Tizi was dirty; it stank of sewers and garbage, and rats infested some of its neighborhoods. Right at five p.m., its women immediately raced back home and double bolted their doors. They busied themselves in the kitchen, surrounded by a snotty-nosed whirlwind of children, while their paunchy husbands calmly read their evening newspapers or watched television and stated every now and then that they were hungry and that their wives should hurry up.

Tizi's women, like those in other cities in this country, sped up when they walked by a café. Why was this place where the males spent entire hours playing checkers or dominos forbidden to them? Women are supposed to have the right to have a cup of coffee after all! And of course, woe betide a woman who might venture to smoke a single cigarette in this region where men not only smoked and chewed tobacco to their hearts' content but also prided themselves on being strong drinkers. But if a woman touched a mere drop of alcohol, the end of the world would surely come and swallow up everything. Yes, that was also Tizi.

But all that aside, Ammi Amar did not want anyone from El Moudja there. Wanted nothing to do with her. Scorned her, lied to her. She suddenly felt like crying, and she didn't know if it was because she had been betrayed or because of the sad fate of the person she thought was her old friend.

"Oh yes, they are a force to be reckoned with," said Warda. "They are watching everyone. And if you cross them, anything might come your way. This poor Amar Dragonfly should have thought of that before dipping his toe into matters beyond him."

When was she going to stop jabbering! Chahira again felt her anger rise as a tear slowly rolled down her cheek. Others threatened to fall; she impatiently held them back. But her panic grew in strength; she felt a strong pressure in her lower belly—it was as if the liquid she had kept from spilling out of her eyes threatened to find an exit through another part of her body. The offensive smell of urine arose, and she felt it rudely spread through the living room and mingle with the aroma of tea and coffee.

Warda vigorously rubbed her nose with a laugh. She had smelled shame, too; that was clear.

"La-hab!" She heard a mocking voice slowly say to her.

The seamstress changed color. She briskly grabbed her handbag and stood.

"You can continue laughing without me," she shot out in a hostile voice. "I have to go."

Dumbstruck, the hostess also stood.

"What's wrong, Chahira? This poor Amar's death really has shaken you. I know you cared for him, but . . . I'm sorry, I didn't mean to twist the knife."

Warda had a worried expression; she seemed sincerely astonished by her friend's anger. Chahira no longer knew what to think.

"Pardon me," she wound up saying, "it's true I liked Ammi Amar a lot. He didn't deserve this . . ."

"Stay a little longer. Let's change the subject. So, this trip to Germany?"

"Austria, not Germany. I'll be back for a final fitting. I have to leave now."

A quick kiss on the cheek, then she hurried toward the door. She gently closed the door as her tears flowed, free at last.

"La-hab!" She heard from behind the door. Warda was snickering again as she said this.

XXIV

There was nothing left to do but admit defeat and submit herself to the yoke of the all-powerful olanzapine. Offer up her mind and energy in order to be rid of the ghosts. Become a zombie once more, aimlessly wandering around, carcass heavy, step slow, eyes deadened. Sell one's consciousness and intelligence to buy a little peace.

Chahira pulled her sunglasses from the top of her head and quickly put them on, as tears had already forced their path, prompted by the bitter weight of defeat and the "enemies" who noisily celebrated in her mind.

"Lahab, you are defeated, defeated!"

This final word's echo was drowned out in an enormous burst of laughter that, gloating in its victory, filled the street but then quickly faded amid the pandemonium of car engines and shopkeepers' calls. It seemed to her that people turned around, curious about this sadistic and incomprehensible laughter. And the *merqouchettes* were not the only ones laughing. Everyone, men and women, laughed; they mauled her from every angle. Their offensive fingers were on her eyelids, on her cheeks, on her lips, on the tips of her breasts, and inside, between her legs. A passerby called out an obscenity. The tears fell ever faster; the sunglasses fogged: she could barely see where she was going.

However, a deep pride mixed in with the tears. For six years, she had held strong. For six years, she had fought against a thousand ghosts, against their thousand voices that assailed her, their profanity, their touching, the jeering and insolent laughter, the intimidation, the smells of sweat, urine, excrement, refuse, blood, alcohol, rotten eggs, and sometimes an indistinct blend of them all. Six years, twenty-four hours a day, without any relief apart from sleep. Six years that she had managed all of this on her own, without medication, continuing to live an almost normal life, in spite of death's constant call. To sew, to do her shopping and to care for herself, to fight against an oppressive submersion. To speak with people fairly politely, though all the while suspecting them of spying and of stealing her thoughts, of provoking her, humiliating her, and laughing at her strangeness. Six years of heroism.

And now, she was, of her own free will, going to beg the doc to prescribe her the very medication she so hated. She herself was going to ask to be transformed into a zombie. In what context had Mr. Rouha said, "It is sad, the hero's defeat?" Those words came to her now with insistence, full of both irony and bitterness.

Then the image of the psychiatrist came to her, smiling, likeable. In spite of her shame, in spite of her defeat, it was not without pleasure that she would go to see him, that tall and charming man in his fifties, to whom she would speak about her troubles as she would a friend. As she would a friend. Really? Chahira suddenly grew angry. At her quickening pulse, at her desire to stop in front of a shop window to fix her hair, at her impatient need to assure herself that she was beautiful and that the tears she had just wiped away had not left any streaks. She frenetically buttoned her jacket and hurried. He must also have been handsome when he was young. And he still was, a little. And that was why she could not talk with him about all those people who taunted her by constantly calling her name, about her tears and fights, and especially about the obscenities and the humiliating smells. Two steps from his office, she panicked.

No, she could not, it would be too shameful. And would he really listen to her? She had a clear memory of her last appointment with him. He had listened distractedly, nonchalantly playing with his ballpoint pen and imperceptibly rocking in his chair. From time to time he laughed loudly, though without any meanness, when she brought up the fight she had had with her sister and her often sarcastic replies. He did not seem to take seriously her belief that people provoked her, that they spoke ill of her, that they paid no more attention to what she said than they would to the ramblings of a child. That was exactly the way he spoke with her: like a well-meaning adult speaking to a disappointed kid.

No, neither he nor the distant and indifferent psychologist nor her own family took her seriously. How could they when they all knew she was insane? The insane, it is well known, have no right to speak; what could they really offer apart from the deliriums that their minds, chaotic and filled with mirages, confused with the truth?

However, it was not all that long ago when the insane were mistaken for saints. People listened to them as they would a revelation, words carrying wisdom and divine knowledge. How everyone in El Moudja venerated Aïcha *El Chouafa!** The old seer's emaciated dark face, small frail body, and halting walk suddenly came back to her memory. People said her extraordinary gift was affirmed when she was barely ten years old. Her father, a domineering man who did not trifle with honor, had decided to marry her off to a prominent man forty years her senior. But the little Aïcha categorically refused to marry this "old guy" she had already seen and found repulsive. As soon as her mother told her this news, she went off to find Si Larbi, the father, in the small village square, ignoring the pleas of her mother, who trembled at the thought of watching a scandal unfold. Before the stunned eyes of those men who were present and whom she had taken as witnesses, she swore to him in a thin but determined voice that this marriage would not take place. That she would kill him with her own hands to prevent it from happening, but that in any case she probably would not need to.

Everyone started to whisper that the poor Aïcha had lost her mind. What other explanation could there be for such scandalous behavior? Her father, for whom nothing—not even insanity—could justify such insolence, began beating her. She did not spill a single tear; she simply gave an enigmatic smile that only revealed its meaning on the day of her marriage, which was planned with great pomp; Si Larbi was not the type to let himself be intimidated by a girl. While they dressed and coiffed the young bride, the father, proud of his brand-new djellaba that curved over his paunchy belly, of the generous amount of meat he had served to his guests during this period of scarcity, and especially of becoming the father-in-law of one of the most

* Aïcha the Seer.

influential men in the region, suddenly fell down in the courtyard amid all his guests, who then got up from their tables, gripped with panic but also irritated at having to stop their banquet.

Nothing much could be done. The obdurate Si Larbi's soul departed a few minutes later, and of course everyone immediately remembered his rebellious daughter's prophecy. And when this girl appeared in the middle of the general lamentations dressed in her most beautiful finery, those present were seized with terror. She seemed to shimmer with an inexplicable aura, all the while giving a calm but triumphant smile that seemed to say, "I did warn him!"

Then everyone bowed before Aïcha's divine insanity; she quickly became Lalla Aïcha. Women and men came from the country's four corners to beg her to tell their future, to ask her advice, or simply to beg for baraka.* The men feared her and treated her as an equal, if not as a superior. The women, who consulted her more frequently, thanked her with endless prayers, carefully prepared meals, pieces of cloth, perfume bottles, or small bars of soap they implored her to accept—Lalla Aïcha did not ask for money—then left her after humbly kissing her forehead. As a child, Chahira had accompanied her mother a few times to the "mrabtiya's";† she still remembered, though vaguely, all those signs of respect.

Oh, if only Chahira's madness had been as venerated as Aïcha's! This highly respected woman did, however, have an atrocious death. It was in 1994, if she remembered correctly; the Bloodthirsty still held the entire country in their hands; these self-proclaimed soldiers of a God they had made in their own image—hideous and cruel—a God they believed they could bribe with dismembered bodies, disemboweled women, and burned babies. One rainy Thursday, she returned home from her boarding school, Lalla Zineb, to learn that the seer's throat had been slit. A dozen angry automatons had broken into the old home where she had always lived; they chanted, "We carry out vengeance, O God, on those who would usurp You." The poor woman, who was in a deep sleep, had no time

---

* *Baraka* signifies "blessing."—*Trans.*

† *Mrabitya* signifies a female marabout, a saintly woman.—*Trans.*

to understand what was going on before they began sliding the knife across her throat and voices from beyond the grave recited some verse from the Quran. She died with a gasp. The Moudjaouis, appalled as they were, concealed their grief. The Bloodthirsty had eyes and ears everywhere; one could never be too careful.

She would have liked to have told the doctor all about this. She especially would have liked to say, "And what if the poor crazy people seated before you were telling the truth? What if they knew more than you? Who are you, with all your self-importance, to declare that my truth is not the Truth?" But of course, she did not say any of this; she was far too tired. She said little. She talked about her move, the loneliness she felt in this city that did not love her in return, the fight with her mother, and the tragic death of Ammi Amar the Aesthete, in whom she saw something of a surrogate father, but one who had betrayed her. She vaguely explained that all these events had completely overwhelmed and weakened her and that she no longer had the strength to keep up the fight without help.

"And the symptoms? Have they gotten better or worse?"

"Worse," she said, exhausted.

And she refused to say any more. The tall man in his fifties asked her if she was sure she wanted to go back on a medication she had not tolerated well a few years before. She feebly nodded as he picked up a pen to write the prescription. After all, did she have anything all that important left to do? She had finished making her pieces for Vienna, and there were not many orders left to finish. Before her flight to Austria, she had almost two months to sleep and sleep some more, since life was nothing but a long waking nightmare.

VIENNA

XXV

Vienna sang, Vienna smiled, Vienna "shared all her charms beneath the July sun." Chahira suddenly remembered this line she had read a long time ago—back when she still read—in a book with an obscure author who had set the story in Paris. "Paris, that mischievous coquette, shared her charms beneath the sun to better entice naive and intimidated migrants." Naive and intimidated: that is exactly how Warda and she felt when they arrived in the cold, yet luminous and gleamingly clean, airport. It was eleven o'clock sharp. And on this day, the national airline, whose legendary delays all her fellow citizens mocked, had demonstrated exemplary punctuality.

"How do we know where to go?" worried Warda. "All the signs are in German or English!"

Chahira wanted to reassure her, to tell her that she still remembered a bit of English from high school. She tried to recall this language's words and grammar—she excelled in it twenty years ago—but she quickly gave up: there was not much left of her knowledge, which even during her time at Lalla Zineb was probably not as great as she imagined it to be.

Yes, how would they know where to go in this futuristic setting that awed them; they who had only seen their own capital a handful of times? They believed it best to follow the other travelers, but in doing so they almost committed a monumental oversight: that of passing through the passport check. Luckily, Ali was there to explain to them that, unlike the other travelers who were mostly members of the European Union, they had to get their travel documents stamped. Then, once they had claimed their baggage, they had to take the escalator to reach the exit. The two women cautiously placed their feet on the mobile walkways, while their new companion kept an attentive eye on them. A sad thought occurred to him: how was it possible that a mechanism as banal as an escalator could, in 2018, amaze his compatriots? His friends hardly came from remote areas of the country; they were from a county seat barely a hundred kilometers from the capital.

They at last reached the top and thought they were through with the experience, when an old gentleman on the step behind theirs suddenly started yelling. Trying to get hold of his crutches in time, he knocked into Warda and sparked a terrible pain in his leg.

"*Das ist nicht nett!*" he repeated angrily.

What did that mean? Was he insulting them? Was he trying to start a commotion? Their trip to Austria was going to start with a scandal!

"Oh, no," Ali laughed, "it's nothing."

He managed to calm the seventy-year-old man with a big smile and a speedy "*Entschuldigen Sie mich,*" then he hurried to accompany the two young women out toward the taxis. Why drag their heavy suitcases through public transportation when the competition organizers were covering their travel expenses?

They had hoped he would go with them on their tour of the city. But he could not. He had to check in with his Austrian model to make sure each outfit fit just as he wanted. He made sure they picked up their room keys and dropped off their bags. Then he quickly explained to them how to take the tramway—which, to the great relief of the seamstress and her model, stopped right in front of their hotel—and quickly showed them a few interesting places to visit.

"But if it works better for you, you can do that tomorrow. I'll be your guide if Gerda's fittings prove satisfactory. See you tonight at dinner!"

He knew Vienna well; he had lived there a few years ago, as he had explained on the plane. He did not share their thirst to discover this world made of lights, which was so different from their own.

*

Chahira did not understand how Warda could prattle on so much in a place like Stephansplatz—Vienna's center—when she had only just discovered it. "Paris, that mischievous coquette, shared her charms beneath the July sun," said that mediocre writer. She had never been to Paris, but she fully wanted to believe that this description suited the French capital, which everyone said was libertine, just like its inhabitants. Yes, Paris was perhaps just as that author described it. But this was decidedly not the impression Vienna gave her. Not at all. Because the splendid Austrian capital did not in any way resemble a *fille de joie,* pretty but debauched. On the contrary, it was every bit a grande dame, just as beautiful as it was distinguished.

While Warda was harping on a shared acquaintance, whom she assailed with feeble gripes, Chahira looked around, not paying the least bit of attention to what her friend was saying. That edifice, with a mercilessly dominant roof that ran its interminable spears into the stoic celestial vault, had to be Stephansdom—St. Stephen's Cathedral—briefly mentioned by Ali. The two-headed eagle, symbol of a now extinguished empire, presided over the side and also appeared to be celebrating some conquest or another. So, was this the Gothic style? And all those other buildings, what was the name for their architectural style, which was less vertiginous, though just as imposing?

She was dying to ask but was sure that Warda, who had about as much interest in art as a newborn had in car racing, would not know the answer. If Ali had been there, he would have told them how baroque architecture had succeeded in the uncertain gamble of reconciling peculiarities, irregularity, and beauty and had triumphed in the seventeenth and eighteenth centuries when, little by little, clergy and princes spoke of their thirst for grandeur and glory in the massive gold-covered, excessively ornamented structures they had built. Yes, Ali would surely have been able to explain all of this, but he was not there. So she contented herself with admiring these imposing buildings that shunned classical rules—still widespread today—that declared elegance necessarily to be found in simplicity and immoderation, and eccentricity only to be vulgar or worthy of derision.

Awed tourists discovered these proud survivors from centuries past via horse-drawn carriages: antiquated streets that, at once cheerful and sleepy, seemed aligned to the shifting moods of that music streaming forth from a distant past. What genius had given birth to this sonorous wonder? Mozart, Strauss,

Schubert? Was this music romantic, classical, or baroque? Of course she could not tell the difference; all she knew was that no other music had penetrated so deeply into her soul as these strange sonorities had, and that in spite of all erudition and refinement characterizing them, they seemed to carry a certain barbarous quality. Though she could not make sense of this analogy, she thought the music had the depth of *Tindi,* that music born in the depths of the Sahara and perpetuated by blue men—and especially women—who were just as imposing as the buildings surrounding her.*

To compare classical music, born beneath Europe's gloom, to the warm and captivating music of the African desert—what a thought! Experts would surely laugh at such nonsense, and with good reason. But this music, which at that very moment was enchanting her ears, bewitched her—captivated her, in fact—just as much as the other did. Was it because both opened to her the doors of a distant and spectacular world so different from her daily existence, which was morose and insignificant?

"Insignificant, insignificant?" Irritated, disapproving voices surged from nowhere. Mohand looked sad. "My music, insignificant?" he seemed to say in reproach.

She shivered. This was the first time in a long time that "the voices" appeared. It had been a month and half, to be precise. She thought she was finally rid of them. That the indomitable olanzapine, magnanimous in spite of its apparent cruelty, once it had numbed her, worn her down, transformed her into the living dead, had at last freed her of her ghosts.

She had taken this accursed prescription for more than a month. Then, fearing she would no longer fit into her ball gown given the weight she had gained and also that she might terrify the Viennese with her lifeless face, she decided to stop taking it, thinking she had been saved: the symptoms had practically disappeared. And now here they were, all coming back without warning. Nacer, the refined one, who could not help but go into a fit of ecstasy before so much elegance; Mohand, the

---

* The designation of "blue men—and especially women" refers to the Tuaregs, a people here identified in connection with their traditional indigo-dyed textiles.—*Trans.*

vexed one, who played the guitar to prove his music was just as good as these complicated compositions which sent her into raptures and into which his own slightly naive songs began to meld; the *merqouchettes,* who were not yet laughing and who shouted their admiration. She was dismayed, dejected; and yet, she was surprised by the joy she felt at coming across these old acquaintances.

"How I have missed you, Mohand! Don't worry, your music has no equal."

Warda brought this mental dialogue to a brisk end.

"How long have I been talking to myself?" Her joking tone camouflaged a very real annoyance.

"I'm sorry. I got carried away by this old decor."

"Have you ever seen anything so beautiful? Look at how posh this all is."

"That's true; it is beautiful. But you know full well I can't rave on about things like you do, Chahira. I keep my head on my shoulders and feet on the ground," the redhead added with a laugh.

"Hey!" she continued, "I think you've caught someone's eye! Look over there!" She elbowed her friend, at once ridiculously excited.

A few meters away, a tall blond man was hoisting tree trunks into some strange kind of vehicle, something like a gigantic dumpster. What exactly was he doing? Was this a cleaning operation? Chahira could not tell. All she knew was that Warda was right. As he worked, the handsome European looked insistently at her, gaze full of admiration, when he was visibly the one who deserved the admiration. She looked at his athletic body, his tanned skin, his strong, attractive arms, and his fair hair that fell heavily on his shoulders; she began to smile. Some looks are precious gifts.

"Well, you can go on back home alone, apparently," she joked. "Looks like I'm staying in Vienna!"

"With a *zebbal,* Chahira? Come on!"*

The forty-year-old was suddenly overcome with disgust. All the wonders that this handsome lumberjack laid before

* *Zebbal:* garbageman, in Algerian dialect.

their eyes had left Warda indifferent. He may have looked like an Apollo, but he was picking up wood and so he was just a *zebbal*—a garbageman worthy of contempt. Chahira never understood how this redhead, who was so tall and beautiful, could be so devoid of aesthetic sensibilities; how she could have such a common personality when she had such a distinguished bearing. Her fiancé, of course, was far from being a *zebbal*. He was a wealthy textile merchant who could barely spell his own name but who was rolling in dough, according to his very own fiancée. What did it matter if he was short and rather mis-shapen? With a shrug, she repeated this to her friends, who repeatedly told her that she was too beautiful for such a man. What would she do at night? Well, the jewelry and beautiful clothing he covered her in made him desirable in her eyes. As our ancestors said, in their great wisdom: *Rrbeḥ yeslilluc*—wealth renders one beautiful.

"I want to go back," the seamstress suddenly said with an anxious voice.

"Now what's wrong?" her friend said with astonishment. "I don't understand you."

No, of course, Warda did not understand. She could not see that a pack of male shadows had risen up with hurled stones and insults to chase off this Austrian who wanted to steal her away from them. She had barely given much thought to the idea that this might have been him, the Klaus she had dreamed about in El Moudja and Tizi. She barely had had enough time to imagine a few moments dancing in this hand-some partner's arms.

"Not on your life!" shouted one of the ghosts in a strong Kabyle accent.

A short brown-haired man suddenly kissed her while caress-ing her hair, defying the others' screams of indignation that lashed out in Kabyle, Arabic, and German. It was a riot in her head. "Klaus" had caused a riot.

XXVI

Ali was the only other Algerian to make it through to the competition's finale. This was not his first time—he had already won two prizes while he was a student at a renowned fashion school in Paris. He remained in the French capital for five years after he had gotten his diploma, then he up and decided to move to Vienna. Why Vienna? Chahira suspected that this tall man with curly hair, bronzed skin, and an easy smile had followed some Austrian lover there, maybe his model, Gerda. But then why had he moved back to Algiers two years ago, devoting himself to creating designs inspired by traditional Algerian clothing but with a modern touch? His dalliance with the beautiful Viennese woman had undoubtedly reached its conclusion, but they had stayed friends, as often happens in Europe but never happened where she was from. Yes, of course, it was always endless hatred and resentment where she was from. Plus, where she was from, friendship between the two sexes remained a strange and suspect thing, even now in the twenty-first century. The only place where mixed friendships bloomed without too much fear or hindrance was on social media. Friendships that were just as superficial as they were virtual . . .

What might this Austrian woman look like? *Gerda* means "female monkey" in Arabic, she thought with a snap of meanness. Now that was a truly ugly name for a woman who was supposed to be beautiful. She was undoubtedly tall and willowy, with delicate features, a pair of blue eyes, and blond, silky hair Chahira imagined to be overly fine. She had been struck by the poverty of soul that the inhabitants of this rich and powerful continent emitted. Their complexion was too sallow, almost washed out; the same was true for their pale eyes that had almost no character: their heads were parsimoniously adorned with hair that was too well behaved, too lifeless; their gait too rapid, too mechanical to be imposing; their speech without emphasis and insufficiently articulate. If her people's soul was rotten and perverted, that of these poor puppets was too pale and nearly absent. Were these people really the descendants of those who had built this magnificent city? Its impressive castles and cathedrals?

"Those people over there aren't Austrian," explained Ali, now looking over at the group of young men and young women she had been staring at for a moment. "Those are tourists—probably English or Irish."

Here again, someone had read her mind. But for once, she did not get angry. How nice it felt to walk with this tall, easygoing young man who was at once confident and affable.

"Yes, I see they're speaking English, even if I don't understand what they're saying."

She went back to watching them. When her people wanted to insist upon someone's beauty, whether it be a man or a woman, they would say the person looked like a *roumi*—a European. Yet neither these English-speaking tourists nor the other passersby seemed beautiful to her. There was something empty, almost dismal, about them. Dismal and ridiculous, these faces were too smooth and shallow; ridiculous, the thin and meager thighs—or the opposite, voluminous and covered in cellulite—stretching out of their tiny shorts. Ridiculous, in the end, all those tattoos and piercings. But of course, she did not dare reveal her thoughts to Ali, who would certainly take her for a *qdima*—a poor woman with old-fashioned tastes from a bygone epoch. A fuddy-duddy who, in addition to no longer being very young, had never left her village and freaked out at a scene as banal as tattoos and bare thighs.

Ali took her and Warda on a pleasant walk through that astonishing and immense amusement park called the Prater, or something like that. They had been there for half an hour, and even though they had yet to try a game, it was entertaining to see all those gargoyles, those gentle monsters, and that fair-like atmosphere. Ali quickly stopped to buy some snacks. At least that was what he claimed. She saw him lean slightly toward the ravishing saleslady, while talking to her in a low voice. She, for example, was beautiful. Her big eyes were a deep blue, and her lips were both supple and plump. Thick blond curls fell like a halo around the curves of her face.

Chahira grew agitated. She did not understand what Ali was saying to the woman, but his voice cooed, and the pretty blonde smiled and slightly bit her bottom lip. She even blushed a little.

"Does it take a century to buy a few miserable snacks?" she almost yelled. But she held herself back, suddenly ashamed of her snide and rather childish jealousy.

Still, Ali was quite the ladies' man! Here was a young man who was just about the same age as her, born barely fifty kilometers from her village, and who seemed to be fully content. How many women had he been with? Dozens, undoubtedly. That was clear from the way he smiled at pretty young ladies, from the perfect ease with which he spoke to them. From the way he whispered sweet nothings to this beautiful saleslady— because that was certainly what he was doing. Why did she not have this same sense of ease? As far back as she remembered, she had been told that a respectable woman owed it to herself to be reserved and grotesquely rigid. A woman who was too re-laxed, too joyful, was automatically a woman with loose mor-als. To be virtuous, one had to be disagreeable, frustrated, and unhappy. Or aloof, as she was sometimes reproached for being.

Yet, there were happy women in her country. Smiling women, women at peace. Women who knew a loving man's gentle words and touch—a man they might leave in order to marry a different one, one imposed upon them by their parents or, quite simply, by good sense. So, resigned and armed with wisdom and beautiful memories, they accepted their fate as women who were ill loved by indifferent and sometimes brutal husbands; as maids reduced to housekeeping and children's education. Of course, some—though they were rare—were luckier: they mar-ried the one they loved, the one who had whispered a thousand sweet words, a thousand promises into their ears. And, by some miracle, the enchantment did not completely dissolve after the wedding.

Enchantment was something secondary for her people, for that matter. They were a people who dreamed so little, she sud-denly thought. Was this the reason she found them to be so sad? To dream, to seek enchantment, is a ridiculous act, and an especially dangerous one that can only lead one astray, especially if that person is a woman. A woman must have her feet planted squarely on the ground. Her ancestors had always mocked women who had their heads in the clouds; in their very appearance, women had to prove that, with their heavy bodies, generous and grounded, they remained attached to the earth by the laws of gravity.

She suddenly recalled Emma Bovary's atrocious end: her deformed body, her bulging eyes, her tongue hanging out. The end of that book, which she had read in her last year of high school when she was barely eighteen, continued to revolt her to this day. "Unfair," she had exclaimed, nervously turning the pages. She had loved that beautiful heroine, who only sought to fight against ugliness and mediocrity. But Flaubert was just like her people, she thought; he did not like women who sought enchantment.

This thought seemed funny to her, and she bit her lip to keep herself from laughing. Warda, who was also strangely silent, seemed lost in gloomy thoughts.

"You are pretty pensive, Warda. It's not like you!"

"No, I'm just a little tired. To tell the truth, I'm a little bored, but I wouldn't dare say that to Ali. I really would have liked to do a little shopping, or at least some window shopping . . ."

"Maybe we'll have the time to do some tomorrow, since the finale isn't until six o'clock. But I don't think we will today. Ali planned to take us to whatever-that-palace-is-called—the one where Empress Sisi lived."

Ali had just left the pretty blonde. He had placed a banknote in front of her; and admiring this graceful move, Chahira, who was still thinking about Flaubert's masterpiece, remembered the passage when Emma, who was two breaths from tragedy and completely ruined by the machinations of Monsieur Lheureux, the fabric seller, found it noble and good to give her very last coin to a beggar.

Ali stepped toward them, all smiles, snacks in hand.

"Here, they are delicious!"

The two women looked at him, grumpy. He quickly apologized, explaining that the young woman—a Czech who had lived in Vienna for a few years—remembered having met him some time before. She was happy to see him again and wanted to tell him all about her recent divorce, her little cherub, who was now two, and her decision to go back to school.

"But mostly about her recent divorce, right?" Chahira thought. She looked at her friends, seized with panic. Hopefully they had not "read" what had just crossed her mind! She would scandalize Ali and thrill Warda, who certainly had had the same idea. Now her thoughts were just like those of that girl she was supposed to despise!

Luckily, Ali—as it was mostly his opinion that mattered, right?—did not seem to have noticed a thing. In a decidedly good mood, he suggested, "Come on, let's do a ride! What do you want to do? The Ferris wheel? The haunted house ride?"

And, in saying this, he placed a friendly hand on Chahira's upper back to encourage her to walk faster. A slight shiver ran through the young woman—such an exquisite feeling! But she quickly stiffened, gripped by an unexpected anxiety. Why had this friendly young man touched her? This act seemed natural and perfectly innocent, but how could she be sure? He had not touched Warda; but he had "allowed" himself with her! She had only herself to blame. It was undoubtedly because of her body, sagging beneath her extra weight, because of this gaze stupefied by years of "insanity" and her exhausting battle against demons. How could anyone respect an unattractive woman with a mindless expression?

XXVII

It was crazy how much Sisi looked like her.

Amid the splendor of the Hofburg Palace, the seat of Habsburgs' glory and power for seven centuries, Chahira certainly admired the luxurious dresses, jewelry, and gilded silver, but she did not linger over them. All that glittered, whether made of gold or not, had never fascinated her unless it was of a human substance: a dazzling gaze, or sleek hair, a smile, or a lively wit. And the empress had it all.

Elisabeth of Bavaria stood before her, imposing despite her pensive gaze. Romy Schneider, though quite ravishing, could not measure up to this peaceful, though slightly melancholy, face's allure. Peaceful. How could it not be when it had that spark and those deep, dark eyes? Certain of its powerful gaze, that face dismissed all necklaces, except for the strand of pearls, its rich color in stark contrast to the bare shoulders and luxurious brown hair. Oh, her extraordinary hair! Legend says her hair fell to her ankles and that it took almost the whole day to wash it, a task the empress assigned to her hairdresser, Fanny Angerer, every three weeks.

Yes, she looked like her. Sure, her hair was far from being as long—it fell to the middle of her back—but it, too, fell in a thick cascade to which the sun hurried to pay homage, weaving its rays into the beautiful auburn hues. And though her complexion was drawn from long years of worry and mental tension, there remained a bit of that spark, that purity she detected in the woman in the portrait and which, at forty, still allowed her to delight in her own appearance, rejecting makeup and jewelry. Lastly, there was the somber and distant gaze—the gaze of someone distracted by dreams of some other place and thoughts that eluded common souls.

She smiled imperceptibly, proud of looking like this woman. However, she suddenly started to worry: the *merqouchettes* would not delay in laughing at her vanity or, worse, giving free reign to their jealousy. They would poke out her eyes, rip off her ears, and make her nose grow. They would break apart her body to destroy her proud bearing; they would grind up different parts of her body to make the most loathsome odors flow forth. But they did not do any of this. These invisible enemies also seemed hypnotized by the portrait's silent charm. It even seemed to Chahira that they were gently nodding their heads, approving of the comparison she had just made.

An admirable woman, this queen for whom beauty was everything, she told herself, ready to plunge once more into her own thoughts. A queen who loved nature, horses, and poems . . . Who wrote them—just like her. Who took such care of her body; who kept a thin and elegant figure until the autumn of her life . . .

A hand furtively tapped her slightly paunchy stomach, while a woman's voice let off a jolting and irritating laugh. The *merqouchettes* had to show up sooner or later, hadn't they! They waited for the perfect moment to attack. Other laughs were quick to follow. They all seemed to say, "You? Look like Sisi with your curves and bulging fat rolls? That's the joke of the century!"

She held herself back from screaming at them to shut up. She wound up telling them in her head: "Not everyone's lucky enough to become an empress. Plus, she didn't take olanzapine; she didn't have the misfortune of knowing you!" The laughter turned into outrage and then cries of protest at this unexpected insult. A new riot threatened to surge.

"A feminist protest," she suddenly heard. That was Nacer, the brains of the group, who—for the first time since she had known him—ventured to joke around a bit. In fact, it was the first time he had distinctly expressed himself.

Chahira quickly stifled her chuckle—half a dozen heads simultaneously looked back at her, half-amused, half-frightened.

"*Nuba n lxalat,* yes!"* she answered, good-humored still. Nacer grumbled in impatience, already seeming to regret his little joke. He uttered no other sound.

---

* *Nuba 'laxalat,* which means "The Women's Show," is the name of a program broadcast between the 1950s and the 1980s on Algerian radio's second channel.

"What a grump!" she replied, vexed. "Yes, being condemned
to live with you is a true curse!"

The force and evident sincerity of this response reduced all
the ghosts to silence. She returned to her train of thought: the
empress had known tragedy. How many loved ones, many in
the prime of their life, did she lose in some terrible way? Chahira
tried to remember their names: her daughter, who died at a very
young age, was named Sophie; and her only son, Rodolphe,
killed himself at barely thirty. And there was her sister, whose
name Chahira no longer recalled, and then the cousin, Louis,
who drowned trying to escape the asylum where he had been
committed. Sisi wept tears of love for him and dedicated one of
her most moving poems to him.

So it was possible to love someone who was insane, someone
with mental illness! Who would weep for her if she died? Her
family, of course—her mother in particular—would manage
to spill a few tears; they would have to make a good impression! Looking like monsters was out of the question! The good
Nouara's tears, if ever she cried, would be more sincere. And
that would be it. They would quickly forget her.

No, she did not really look like this empress after all. What
a stupid idea to compare herself with her. The *merqouchettes*
were right to make fun of her. Their worlds were too different.
In her world as an Algerian seamstress, there were no palaces or
horses or cruises or loving parents or even a prince charming—
well, an emperor charming—or . . .

How could this woman remain such a worried and melan-
cholic soul while she was loved by everyone—from her happy
childhood at Possi, in Bavaria, to her coronation as queen of the
Hungarians, who spontaneously pledged her their allegiance, so
great was their love for her? There had been the imperial pro-
tocol to which she had to bend, and the occasional annoyances
due to her mother-in-law; but in the end, who would take that
seriously if not a young, spoiled empress? Far too used to being
loved and to seeing all her wishes come true?

"*Nyants*—they killed her," Nacer quickly told her.

It was true. This adulated woman—how ironic is fate—was
assassinated. If destiny shows itself to be just as ironic with me,
I'll probably know unparalleled glory after my death!

The *merqouchettes* laughed. Nacer and Mohand too. A young man whose name she did not know applauded. She smiled, pleased with her sense of self-derision.

"Why are you smiling?"

The smile on Warda's lips when she asked this question became even more radiant. She was visibly delighted at having visited a part of the palace with the charming Ali.

"Ah, here you are again!"

"Don't tell me you haven't moved from this spot." The young man was surprised. "Warda and I have seen so many interesting things—dishes, gymnastic equipment, the private carriage—and here you are, still staring at that portrait!"

Don't you think she looks like me? She almost asked. But she held back; it would be too ridiculous.

"I find the portrait admirable," she said simply. "And the woman too."

Ali gave a blunt and sonorous laugh: "Well, there's nothing to say about the portrait; it is indeed admirable. As for the woman . . ."

"You don't like Sisi?" Regret and astonishment fused in her hesitant voice.

"Oh, I can't say I don't like her," replied the other with a wink. "A woman this beautiful! But I think her history's been too romanticized, too idealized. Westerners know how to do this so well. After all, did she really do anything that significant? In the end, she was a woman who couldn't have been any more traditional: a beautiful woman, wife, and mother who accepted that her husband had mistresses, even though some say she succumbed to a temptation or two herself. I think feminists shouldn't care much for her!" He let out his beautiful laugh, winking again.

Feminists. Why are they all using this word today? She was aggravated that in one fell swoop he had tarnished the sublime image she had had in her mind. She wanted to say, *But she loved Beauty!* She did not dare say anything, however. Ali, so full of glib assurance, slightly intimidated her.

He suddenly looked at her with insistence. "It's funny to say this, but you know you look like her a bit? Same coloring, same somewhat distant gaze . . . On the other hand, you're doing something meaningful, unlike her! You make your own designs; you're the ambassador for what is beautiful in your country . . . And if you are here in Vienna, it's due to your own merit!"

She blushed with delight. She thought confusedly that Sisi also wrote poems and that she was very good on horseback; that she became queen of Hungary on her own and not thanks to her husband . . . But in the end, what did it matter? Already, Ali was whispering something tender in her ear; already, he was caressing her temple; already . . .

"I think Warda is bored," he said, gently touching her shoulder, pulling her from her sweet reverie. "Shall we go walk by the Danube?"

XXVIII

"I'm telling you to kiss my mother's forehead!" repeated Ali, unbending.

"And I'm telling you that I can't. Sorry."

She saw him change color. A moment before, he had been all sweetness, all kindness. She had loved his beautiful words softly whispered in her ear; she had loved the way his broad hand caressed her hair; she loved feeling his strong arm around her waist as they etched out a few waltz steps. Yes, he had been perfect up until the moment he had introduced her to *Yemma* Rabha, his mother. She had tried to express how much respect she had for her and that she would gladly kiss her cheek; he would not be dissuaded. That kiss on the forehead had become an obsession.

She did not see coming the first slap, full of hate and icy. She only felt its effect when the ghosts all at once uttered a terrorized scream.

"What's going on?" she asked them, irritated.

She had just started to feel the heat from her bruised cheek when they screamed again. An intense pain in her lower belly overtook her, as did a strong urge to vomit. She felt numb but now understood her invisible guests' appalled silence: what followed the slap was a most brutal rape. She nearly blacked out.

Her parents, pale and terrorized, stood docilely before him. He made fun of their humble posture and said the most dishonorable things to them.

"Leave my family alone!" She tried to use a firm, convincing voice, but she trembled despite all her efforts.

"Kiss my shoe," he ordered the old Rabéa.

"No, *Yemma*," she yelled with all her force in her mind. "Don't do it!"

But the mother moved toward him like an automaton and started lowering herself.

Hani leaped from nowhere and, shoving her mother aside before she completely humiliated herself, approached the monster, eyes full of rage, and delivered a blow and spat in his face.

Chahira mentally clapped her hands: "Bravo, my brother, I'm proud of you, *ya sbaa!*"* Kader and Rabéa smiled weakly. She felt an intense love blooming inside her; an intense and un-rivaled love for this family which was hers. Tears flowed while she hugged her old parents, after having patted her younger brother on the shoulder in that cool way young people do.

She saw her brother suddenly lurch forward. The monster had kicked from behind. Furious, Hani stood, turned around, and kneed him in the stomach. The other howled then stiffened, seeming to give up the fight. His face had changed: his mouth curled into an incomprehensible smile, and then he settled a strange, hypnotic gaze upon his adversary, who held him by the collar. Hani let him go, arms suddenly lifeless and eyes empty, like those of a zombie. She screamed again in her head, but the nightmare was only beginning.

She saw her brother, now a larva, docilely endure other abuses, other degradations, other horrors, right before her parents' paralyzed stare . . .

She began to whimper, rocking her huddled body back and forth, as she did each time she was distressed, and nervously blinking her eyes to chase away these monstrous images. Her ghosts, the *merqouchettes* included, looked at her with full sympathy, even though they were too frightened to show it. At last, Mohand timidly came closer and brushed her cheek with uncharacteristic gentleness. He smiled. She threw herself into his arms, overcome with uncontrollable tears.

She suddenly got ahold of herself and quickly wiped away her tears: someone had just knocked at the door. She carefully splashed water on her face and dried it before opening the door, hoping her fit of crying had not left a trace. She slowly opened the door, trying to regain her composure.

* I'm proud of you, lion!

Ali stood before her with his tall, carefree figure and his charmer's smile. She instinctively stepped away.

"What's wrong, Chahira? Something's wrong; you are completely pale." His smile froze, and his tone of voice betrayed a real concern.

"It's nothing," she answered, forcing a smile. "I'm just tired. And mostly I'm really stressed out about tomorrow."

"Oh, you shouldn't be. It's not a matter of life or death, you know!" He returned to his lighthearted tone. "Listen, Chahira, someone called for you down at reception—your mother, I think. I'd just returned and asked for my key, but the receptionist was on the phone. He was repeating your name and room number. I told him that if it was a call for you, I'd deliver the message. They're going to call in ten minutes; it might be best to head straight down."

XXIX

Hani was lying there, a few steps from her, motionless, drool-ing, tongue hanging out, eyes rolling. Ali had turned him into a dog, a larva, a mop. He had fought bravely, but his enemy had the seeds of Evil within—he *was* Evil. For an hour, she had struggled not to see him undress, wipe up the excrement of his laughing executioner, kiss his feet, and his bottom. Once, twice, a hundred times. She wished she could have fainted, or even died. But it must have been written somewhere that she had to go to the very end of this horror.

"Enough, enough!" She shocked herself by begging the mon-ster, "Spare my brother, I beg of you."

Degraded, traumatized, she was nothing more than a human rag—barely in better shape than her brother. Arms wrapped around her knees, which she had pulled up to her chest, she moaned, her whole body trembling. The monster held on, sa-voring his crushing victory, arms crossed, mouth twisted into a scornful smile.

Mohand consoled her at first.

"Your brother is truly brave," he told her. "He did not disap-point us."

He put his hand on her shoulder. But she leaped away, fright-ened, and whimpered even louder. So he put his arms down. When she saw him moving away from her, her mind fell into complete darkness. Aïcha the Seer's decapitated body lay there, next to her brother's, while her bloody head reigned from a few steps away. Then other heads emerged, those that the Blood-thirsty had scattered throughout El Moudja's narrow streets more than twenty years ago.

Mohand returned; he had brought his guitar. She had always loved listening to him play. But there was no way for that to happen here. She retched. Mohand thought he was doing the right thing, but it was in disappointingly bad taste. She gently pushed him away.

What else was there to do? There was no possible escape. She suddenly remembered her first attack: the night when her illness erupted without warning. The first voyeurs who watched from behind the walls as she got undressed, the first touches, the first spied on and stolen thoughts. On that day, she had understood that she had to, as soon as possible, put an end to a life that promised nothing but suffering and, more importantly, degradation. It was not a desire; it was a duty. She had even tied a long scarf to the short lightbulb string in the bedroom; she had then tied a sturdy knot. She had climbed up on a chair and, banishing the ghosts' distraught screams and the *merqouchettes'* nervous cries, had placed her head through the knot. But nausea had struck her the moment her chin touched the cord, and she quickly got down from the chair once she had freed her head.

No, she could not do it—not like that. She had to find another way. Delirious, she raced to her computer and searched the best ways to end one's life. That was how she found the story of that Virginia—that British writer whose last name she no longer recalled. If she remembered correctly, it was an animal name. Virginia Fox or Wolf, or something like that. She found her admirable, this woman who was so maligned by her hallucinations that she chose to depart before she lost full control over her mind and life. Her solution was quite simple. She filled her pockets with stones and let the river that neighbored her home swallow her.

It was a beautiful death—serene and not too slow. Ever since that sinister night, how many times had her mind returned to that Virginia, promising herself that she would follow in her footsteps, though she never had the courage to do so? But now was the time: this could not continue. Like the illustrious English woman, she would let herself be swallowed up by water, the Danube's blue water. She had seen the famous river the day before and knew it would do the trick. With rocks in her pocket, she would drown herself before ever realizing she had gone in; and those stupid Europeans would be so busy making out or showing off their bottoms and their withered breasts that they would not notice a thing. They would let her be. She sighed with relief at the thought. Yes, she would be gone for good. Oh, yes, it would be a beautiful death! Surrounded by greenery and water in the heart of glorious Vienna. A foretaste of paradise.

Layali el uns fi Vienna
Nasimha min hawa el ganna . . .

She probably would not be allowed into the real one—the real Beyond—but all the same! What better end could she hope for, the unknown seamstress from El Moudja, a lost corner of the Third World? Was she not a hundred times luckier than that poor Emma, disfigured by arsenic and ruined by one of the ugliest deaths, when beauty was all she ever lived for? She was relieved and, on the whole, happy.

To leave, to leave, to rest at last. When? Tomorrow? No, the day after tomorrow, once the competition's finale concluded.

Mohand quickly put down his musical instrument.

"You will win," he whispered, pleased to find a good reason for her to forget about her wicked plan.

She merely shrugged. She had even lost interest in this competition. She would participate only out of principle because she had committed to it. But in truth, it would be magnificent to leave with a victory . . .

"What did they say on the phone?" Mohand tried again. "Is it why you're like this now?"

How could Mohand ask such a stupid question when he had seen it with his own eyes? How could he suggest that the telephone was the reason she thought about ending it, when he had witnessed all the horrible things she had been through.

Who was on the phone? Her mother, of course. She had called to tell her that her father had been hospitalized. His blood pressure had skyrocketed.

"How is he now?" she asked, more agitated than ever.

"He was semiconscious for a long time. He finally came to, *hamdoullah*. He just asked to see you, but of course, you're off 'dancing' in Europe—or doing God knows what else. And he hasn't stopped crying since. He keeps repeating, '*Waalach benti?* Why, my daughter?'"

The young forty-year-old also started to cry: "I haven't done anything, *Yemma,*" she repeated feverishly. "I haven't done anything!"

"Don't tell me you haven't done anything, Chahira. What you have put your poor father and me through is too much to bear. You're the reason we are in this difficult situation, living in shame. And now we don't dare raise our heads up high to anyone. *Bahdeltina, hramaalik!*"[*]

The tears that reached Chahira from the other end of the line would have—under different circumstances—seemed overplayed, fake to her. But on that night, she did not want to waste time on such details. She had made her old father cry, and her mother was certain they were tears of shame.

"I haven't done anything. I haven't done anything!" she repeated, over and over, continuing to cry. "What shame are you talking about, *Yemma?*" she finally thought to ask. "Don't speak of shame, I beg you!"

"What shame am I talking about?" Rabéa asked with a tired voice. "When have you ever been a normal girl, like everyone else? How many years have we put up with you? Then one day, you leave, just like that, slamming the door behind you. You think the neighbors haven't noticed your absence? That they thought nothing of it? *Ou mazal ou mazal.*"

The woman, thus accused, kept silent, breathless. What should she say? That she was sorry? She would have liked to, but it did not want to come out. Because, deep inside, she continued to tell herself she had done nothing wrong.

"*Ou mazal ou mazal:* and there is so much more," her mother had concluded. The insinuation was all too clear. The shame she had inflicted upon them was not the decision to live alone nor was it that she traveled alone in Europe, both of which had fed the gossip mill. The real shame, the one Rabéa did not dare mention, was the other one—that of Hani enduring the worst disgraces because of that monstrous lover he had met in Vienna; that of the permanent touching that had made both her and her family the laughingstock of the neighborhood; that of the innumerable ghost lovers she wound

[*] You've thrust shame upon us; how cruel of you to do this to us.

up giving in to. Yes, she was an unworthy girl, a hussy. Yes, she had brought shame to her family and especially to her old father, who had been sick for years. Yes, she had to die. Even if she did not deserve the death she had planned; it was too beautiful for her.

XXX

Wael Waraqa had lived in Great Britain for nearly ten years and had already sparked spirited debates in Saudi Arabia with his "daring" creations inspired by Saudi traditions. Chahira had read online that he had already won a prize in the United States with a "modern" and "secular" version—these were the terms the Western press used to describe and praise it—of the long *abaya* women wore in his country. The traditional black of this revisited *abaya* had been broken up by a large pink scarf casually knotted around the waist. No scarf, however, over the head; the famous Scottish top model Shirley McLaureen, who was none other than his wife, had her hair freely flowing over her shoulders. This time, Waraqa was suggesting nothing short of dressing women . . . in men's fashion! Shirley McLaureen was divine in the beige *qamis* that, without having too much fabric taken in, followed the delicate curves of her svelte body and fell a few centimeters below the knee. On her head, she wore a beige *keffiyeh,* but the *agal*—the traditionally black doubled "wheels"—were in a sky blue, as were her strappy sandals.

There was nothing to say: it was ingenious and absolutely ravishing, thought Chahira. But this was the type of clothing most likely to appeal to Western judges. At least that is what Ali said—the Ali of tangible reality, not the monstrous and sadistic shadow born in her head—during their conversation on the plane. Chahira started to imagine herself also becoming a famous designer and being interviewed all around the world. Would people then accuse her of being a traitor and in the pocket of the West if she voiced all of her hatred for the scarf and her country's hackneyed and pestilential traditions? What choice would she make then? Refuse to critique everything she had always abhorred out of fear of looking like a sellout and a puppet of those who ruled the world? Betray her own ideas rather than betray her people?

What stupid questions! She would never encounter this dilemma. Then the *merqouchettes* laughed, as all sorts of voices repeated in unison: "Danube, Danube!"

"Yes, the Danube is waiting for me. I'm not backing out," she responded in her head with resentment.

She had not, in effect, changed her mind; the plan she had made the day before had not left her. However . . . however, something within her hoped that some *je ne sais quoi* would render her plan useless, even ridiculous. Yes, inside she still naively hoped for a miracle . . .

"Can you give me a little break, just for this evening?" After a moment, she mentally added, "Please."

Then the voices fell silent. Not for the whole of the evening, of course; that would have been too perfect. But Chahira was able to calmly watch the whole fashion show—or almost all of it.

The Saudi designer and his wife had competition. Oustina Ivanova was a towering creature with cold blue eyes and abundant brown hair. She walked down the runway, which was so highly polished that you could see your own reflection in it, with an assured walk and the overly serious face of top models accustomed to spotlights and the most prestigious fashion magazines. Later, Chahira would learn that at barely twenty-one years old, she was a true star in Russia—her native country—and that she had begun making a name for herself around the world.

This Oustina was beautiful, and when Chahira saw her walk, she knew that she and Warda would not win the final. It had to be said that the outfit was as beautiful as the model. The designer, a certain Macha Malakova, had the ingenious idea of putting jeans together with traditional Russian wear. Well, this certainly was not the most imaginative of the competition, but . . . Malakova, she made a garnet *sarafane* that could not have been more classic, but it was considerably shortened so it fell only to the hips. Enhanced by the traditional white shirt, it was worn with jeans that curved over the model's slender long legs and were embellished with small floral patterns similar to arabesques and embroidered with gold thread—in the way of a caftan. On her head, Oustina wore a *kokochnik*—the traditional Russian headpiece—on which the understated garnet went with the *sarafane,* her wooden-soled clogs, and the small handbag worn across her chest, which was also subtly embroidered with gold thread. Chahira found the whole of it to be at once novel and of a dazzling beauty. The Russian candidate had every chance of winning too.

But she could just as easily place her bet on the yellow and black mini-*boubou* by the Senegalese Boubacar Diouf; it was worn by a model who had been made impossibly tall with a high hairstyle and stiletto heels, which were also yellow. Why did she find this Awa Kane sublime, she who—like all her people—swore by light skin? Why could she not take her eyes away from her lofty stature and intense and elusive gaze? She saw Black people all the time in Tizi N'Tlelli, but she had never found them attractive. They had pleading looks, defeated faces, and dusty feet; they tirelessly held out their chapped hands, repeating "*Sadaqa fi sabil Allah*"* in an accent many found comical rather than moving. Some men—often ones who surely thought themselves to be benevolent—entertained themselves by jokingly repeating the unfortunate supplication. For their part, the young sub-Saharans also grew bolder over the course of time. They harassed passersby, touching their arms, grabbing onto their hems. Chahira gave them a coin every now and then, but she could not hold back a slight fear of them. She did her utmost to avoid them and sometimes walked on the other side of the street when she saw them.

No, these poor creatures were not pleasant to see. And yet . . . she suddenly thought about Warda's words the other day when she was trying to justify her choice of husband: *Rrbeḥ yeslilluc*—wealth renders one beautiful. She tried to imagine what these dirty snotty-nosed little Africans would have looked like if they had been clean, well-fed, and well-dressed. If fate had been on their side. She also tried to imagine this magnificent Awa's childhood. Perhaps she had grown up in misery and war, as had so many kinky-haired people who populated this

---

* Set phrase frequently used by beggars and that might be translated as: "Give alms, for the love of God."

rich but ill-fated continent; perhaps people told her again and again that she was ugly, making fun of her charcoal-colored skin, of her never-ending legs, and—if those making fun of her were particularly cruel—of her woolly hair. Yes, she had heard such stories where the ugly duckling is transformed into a black swan, an icon of elegance; anyway, ebony sirens winning beauty pageants was as much in style as praising to high heavens "repentant" Muslims or, at the very least, those won over by Western values. Well, of course, good for them, those gazelles—and for those adulated Muslims, too, if what they expressed reflected their own convictions. But why was it that every time she tuned in to a program on a French station—something that did not happen very often—she found all these beautiful words glorifying tolerance, difference, and equality to be hollow and artificial? They came up so often that they bothered her. Unless it was the fad that bothered her. After all, it was normal to grow weary of things everyone says, perhaps mechanically, without much conviction.

A grumbling began. The masculine voice only she could hear seemed to want to say that everything bothered her, for that matter. She stiffened, anticipating the laughter of malevolent ghosts, but silence fell immediately. She sighed in relief. It was true that almost everything exasperated her. Though she had so many complaints against her compatriots, she could not manage to trust this Europe, despite its impressive ancient buildings, its intimidating modernity, and the soft air of freedom that envelops you as you walk through its clean streets, smiling even through the gloomy weather.

She suddenly smiled. A fashion designer—since this was pretty much what she was, even if she did not have a diploma to prove it—who was so bothered by the word *fashion*. How ironic! Awa Kane disappeared the moment she said this to herself. The irony—that of destiny—could sometimes be rather gentle, as it was for this Black siren for whom she had invented a joyless childhood. But her own destiny had selected another type of irony—a tragic irony, she would undoubtedly have thought, if only she had been familiar with this expression.

Her thoughts strayed less as she watched the models that followed. The Indian designer was of a very brown elfish variety, and his glasses were the most prominent aspect of his small round head. What was his name again? Vogadour or Vayabour, something like that. She quickly gave up trying to remember his name; in any case, she thought the little multicolored sari his model with shriveled-looking eyes wore was ridiculous; the model had a markedly reluctant sort of walk, as if she had been forced to be there and was rushing to get it over with.

Then it was Ali's turn. He had disappeared some time earlier to make sure his model was completely ready. And now, oh, what a surprise, he walked side by side with the tall Viennese woman as if he also had been a model his whole life. Gerda was almost as Chahira had imagined: a tall blonde with blue eyes and straight, thin hair. But she walked with admirable ease in a type of trendy *karakou:* as well as having the cut of this traditional garment from Algiers—a collared, fitted jacket that followed the chest's contour and a flat pair of pants with slits on either side—the whole outfit was done in a deep green fabric that was much more subdued and lighter in weight than the velour usually associated with it. No pearls or gold thread on this cotton-polyester blend: there was only thin white embroidery around the collar and sleeves. Next to her, Ali, sharing his magnetic smile with the audience, walked triumphantly in baggy pants and a long-sleeved shirt with a slightly raised collar. Unsurprisingly, this outfit was paired with a burnoose—white like the rest of the outfit. Echoing his partner's *karakou,* the designer had used some green lacing as a belt and also to wrap around the sleeves. The result caused a sensation. Captivated, the audience gave a standing ovation to the cold blonde-haired woman and the extroverted dark-haired man.

Extroverted and also audacious, but mostly quite clever. The competition was supposed to have been reserved solely for women's wear; so in theory, only the garment worn by Gerda Stolz could be judged. But the handsome man from Algiers knew that the impression of the whole was what mattered: an impression that his stylish look and conquering smile could only work to his advantage. Plus, the spectacle of this "Oriental" man—this dark-haired man with the conquering smile, as the song would have it—walking arm in arm with a pale European woman epitomized the competition's theme: a marriage of roots (*tradition,* in other words) and the modern world that, for the jury, could only ever mean something Western.

"That devil," she told herself, watching him slip away with his beautiful woman and thinking confusedly about the mental tortures he had inflicted upon her the night before. He is going to win; I am sure of it. It will either be him or the Saudi.

*

She could not discern any sign of admiration in the audience when Warda walked the runway in her mid-length *fouta*-like skirt, black top with *amendil*-like fringe, and coral necklace. There was no fascinated silence like that which had marked Awa Kane's and Oustina Ivanova's walks. With her svelte body, fine features, and flamboyant hair, the redhead from Tizi N'Tlelli had, however, no reason to envy them. Or perhaps she did: she did not have that fierce air or that distant, impenetrable gaze. She did not have that lofty *je ne sais quoi* in her bearing or facial expressions. Was this the reflection of her ordinary soul? Or was it simply because she was not a professional model and had not been initiated into this savoir faire they dispensed in an Occident that—it is well known—leaves nothing to chance? Oh, the audience showed exemplary politeness. They kept from chattering or looking somewhere else as the beautiful Tizean woman walked, if a bit stiffly, down the runway; but Chahira was no fool—she was convinced they were only pretending to be interested in her outfit.

But the worst came when the emcee announced the designer's name at the end of her walk. As soon as they heard her say "Chahira Lahab," the entire audience turned in their seats. A short stubby journalist took off his large glasses and held them theatrically against his lower belly; a tall blond with a malicious look stuck out his tongue and appeared amused as he stared at her; Macha Malakova scratched her palm hard, blinking all the while. All this was intolerable, and they knew it. That was why they did it.

She felt Malakova's wet sex on her lips; she had not experienced this type of sensation since the fights she had had with her sister a long time ago. Trying to get away, she heard her own mental grumbling. An uncontrollable laughter rang throughout the room. Had they heard the shameful sound she had made, or was it that her appearance was grotesque? Yes, she suddenly felt grotesque in the beautiful dress she had been so proud of when she patiently and caringly created it. Had she not promised herself she would outshine all these insipid Europeans with her presence and elegance? So why then did she now feel so hemmed in and graceless? The very thought of putting on such a dress now seemed ridiculous to her. Most of the women had, of course, dressed up, but in the style of the twenty-first century, not that of a bygone era! She shifted in her seat, head sinking into her shoulders, on the verge of tears. She wanted to disappear, die. Oh well, that was for a little later; tomorrow was very close. That thought consoled her some.

From out of nowhere, Ali's hand came to rest gently on her shoulder. "That was good," he said with a wink. "You know you have every chance of winning?"

"Bravo," said Malakova, with a little smile, her tic having suddenly stopped.

But they were already announcing the next contestant. Silence fell once more.

XXXI

Then there was the waltz, the greatly anticipated waltz. When the fashion designers and their models entered the room, exclamations rang out everywhere. They were not, however, in one of the Austrian capital's famous salons—those of the Hofburg castle she had visited the day before, or of the opera, for example: traditional balls were only held in winter. But the Rathaus—the city hall—was also a splendor, as this large ballroom proved with its neo-Gothic style, all arches and vaulted ceilings, its thousand lights, and immaculately white statues. In this sumptuous room, those who had been born with a silver spoon in their mouth—or those who were lucky enough to find one along life's bumpy road—came to take part in the Saint-Sylvester ball for a few hundred euros. Of course, the glitz was less evident on this July day. The dress code was less strict, and the orchestra was less seasoned. That said, never had Chahira—nor undoubtedly the majority of the fashion designers present at this competition's finale—ever hoped of tasting such luxury. The glum Moudjaouie, though, only paid vague attention to the beautiful decor surrounding her. She had mechanically followed the crowd into the ballroom, mind elsewhere, lost in the memory of her latest humiliation.

Ali walked by, arm in arm with Gerda.

"You look splendid in this dress," he said with conviction.

He seemed completely sincere, but Chahira was sure he only said this because he could sense her consternation. Out of pity, in fact. And that this handsome, dark-haired man who was so sure of himself looked at her with pity—however well-meaning—was even more mortifying, more painful than everything else she had endured that evening.

Warda acted especially kind too.

"What's wrong, Chahira? I disappointed you. I am truly sorry if I was not on the same level as everyone else. I did my best, I promise."

Chahira forced herself to smile. "No, you were really great, Warda. Thank you for everything you have done to help me. We both worked so hard."

"To finish eighth out of fifteen in a competition of this size," Ali interjected, having overheard their conversation, "is a real honor. And without ever having taken a class in fashion design or in modeling! Bravo, my ladies, truly. I think I'd like to work with you both . . . Would you ever consider moving to Algiers? I know we can't discuss this now. Maybe tomorrow, over breakfast?"

Fräulein Stolz had been listening to him up until then with a slightly dumb smile, which contrasted with the aura she had had during her walk; but then she started acting impatient and even began gently pulling on her friend's arm.

"You'll have to excuse her bad mood," Ali said. "She's upset at having missed the podium by so little."

"I completely understand. But fourth, it's marvelous. You'll be on the front page when you get back to Algiers!"

She interrupted a quiet laugh that had immediately seemed odd to her own ears, and added, "In any case, we expected those results. No surprises there. There was little doubt that the Saudi would win."

Ali snuck a look around, hoping the Saudi in question was not in earshot. Chahira stopped talking, confused. What she said was true. Waraqa had married a European woman and liked to imagine himself as subversive; his victory was hardly a surprise. Westerners really like these Orientals—the type that embraced their ideals. Just as predictable was the second-place award given to Boubacar Diouf and Awa Kane, the Black beauty who served up the tough and potentially futile vision of tolerance and togetherness. And there was undoubtedly a political or ideological reason for Gandhi's double—the Indian fashion designer whose name she could not recall—to take third place, since he and his multicolored sari were just as ridiculous as his model. Yes, certainly, because Chahira could barely fathom this duo's work meriting a place on the podium, coming in two

places before the breathtaking Oustina who, with Macha Malakova, only placed fifth, right behind Ali Elkhir and Gerda Stolz.

"Because Gandhi!" guffawed a ghost in her head.

She told herself in passing that this quip was less crazy than
it seemed, with Gandhi being something of another incarnation
of the good "Oriental," wise and pacifist. But she was too overcome by all the instances of upset and anguish that the Problem
inflicted upon her, and she heard herself scream inside her head
at this intruder: "Shut it!"

A dozen pairs of eyes fell upon her, surprised or questioning,
as silence once again fell. They had again heard her anger, even
if she had not said anything. She was exhausted. So exhausted!

*

Ali held her very close to calm her down. He wrapped his
strong arms around her waist, as if that were the most natural
thing in the world, or as if their lives depended upon it. She
felt his chest brush against her chest and his breath so close to
her face, and an indescribable panic took hold of her. She tried
to calm down: *Relax for once; let yourself live.* Then quickly,
without interruption and with insistence: *Relax, relax, relax.*
It did not work: she could not do it. Her hand, rigidly set on
her partner's imposing shoulder, hurt. She was undoubtedly
hurting that of the man from Algiers too: did she not see him
wince in pain, pain he unsuccessfully attempted to conceal behind a smile? Yet that smile grew more and more forthright as
the rhythm of the dance accelerated and she struggled to keep
up. The young man, more and more at ease, lifted her off the
ground, spinning her around, while she awkwardly followed,
ashamed at feeling so wanting of lightness and grace.

The violins' lament finally ceased, and Ali set her back down
as if he were getting rid of a tree trunk he had had to carry. Yes,
that was what he felt, she was sure of it, she read it on his face
once again.

"*Es war wunderbar!*" he said with theatrical flourish.

What was that? Undoubtedly some kind of compliment; but
Chahira knew full well that he did not believe a word of it. Already he had left her to rejoin his Gerda, after giving her a smile

full of gracious condescension that killed her. And then, why had he spoken in German? Only to mark his superiority, something she was only too aware of. In El Moudja and even in Tizi, she had felt beautiful and even rather cultivated . . . and now she was on the ground, completely devastated. Because now Gerda was looking in her direction with the same smile of disdain and indulgence.

When her second dance partner, the tall blond with a lilting accent, approached her, she had already started to smell sweat deviously emerging from her body. She was certain two gigantic sweat rings adorned her underarms; and even if the fingers she subtly ran under them emerged completely dry, the feeling remained. The rest would follow soon enough: a thousand odors unfurling, a thousand voices assaulting her, a thousand hands coming to interfere with her movements and dance steps. Escape! She had to escape! But that was impossible. So she forced herself to smile at that big strong man standing before her, hoping for a waltz. Klaus! Was this him? Yes, Klaus was finally there. He looked just like the one she had imagined while she dreamed, listening to Asmahan's song. Well, a little. True, this Klaus had blond hair rather than chestnut brown, and his hairline was slightly thinning, despite his youth—he probably was not any older than thirty-six years old. But he had the same sweetness in his blue eyes, the same tall stature, the same mildly embarrassed smile.

"*Ich heiße* Karl," he said quickly. "*Und Ihnen?*"

More tense than ever, she smiled again. Karl, Klaus, what was the difference? She might at last dance the gorgeous waltz of her dreams. Where had he come from? She did not remember having seen him in the days before, nor earlier during the competition.

But the dance was already starting. And already, the odors were letting loose; already the groans were multiplying. She felt confined as the other solid arm circled her waist. A dark-haired man. A blond-haired man. In the space of the same evening; in the space of a few minutes. "*Bahdeltina, hramaalik,*" her mother said over and over. Her father cried tears of shame, repeating, "*Waalach benti?*"* Ali placed one hand then the next

---

* The first expression, for which the author provides an earlier note, signifies: "You've thrust shame upon us; how cruel of you to do this to us." The second signifies: "Why my daughter?"—*Trans.*

on her back, her shoulder, her chest, while snickering. Warda was snickering too.

She was the most common of whores. Expressions of disgust rang out from everywhere.

"Slut! Bitch!" shouted a voice.

The *merqouchettes,* also disgusted, opted gradually to distance themselves, while the stench of sweat grew ever more offensive. As dull, but virtuous, matrons, they had to avoid this shameless woman's company. She suddenly froze, unconsciously letting go of this "Klaus's" hand. He looked at her, shocked by this unexpected action.

"*Sorry,*" she said, going red up to her ears. That was one of the few English words that remained from her years in high school.

"Klaus" gently put his hand in hers, and they started to dance again, he with his light and assured movements and she with a growing discomfort that slowly transformed into pain. She now saw the Austrian's serene smile become a grimace; disgust had taken him over as well. How could this have unfolded in any other way? The stench of sweat now became intolerable, and even she was gripped with nausea. She put her arms down to forestall this unwelcome odor; then she felt her stomach expand and swell. Other strange smells followed: a blend of flatulence and cooked meals. How could she mask these aromas of shame? And, more importantly, how could she continue to dance when her whole body had gone rigid?

"*Sorry!*" she cried out again, her face crimson.

She had just stepped on Karl/Klaus's feet. The Austrian seemed exasperated, eager to be done. His expression of sweetness was gone. He stopped a moment and conspicuously pinched his nose. Chahira saw that he had a mocking grin. When they started the dance again, his movements seemed to his partner to be without delicateness and deliberately brusque. Then the violins fell silent once more. Klaus immediately walked off without glancing back at her. He laughed heartily as he headed toward a couple of friends; meanwhile, she fought back her tears.

XXXII

Tomorrow, the Danube will take me in its arms.

All night long she repeated those words, like a child repeating his little poem to recite it well at the end-of-year celebration. Tomorrow, the water will make me its own; it will envelop me in its beautiful blue taffetas, it will lay its ochre jewelry upon me, and enthrone me as queen of its mysteries. Water only ever welcomes queens. Asmahan, the Druze princess, but also the queen of jade and nightingales, who perished in the Nile's waters, killed perhaps by the British with whom she was allied. Virginia, the unrivaled queen of the pen, who chose to escape her demons, selecting a home in the depths of a small river—the one bordering her country home—while that glorious London was being bombed by other demons emerging from Germany. And then Ophelia, the sweet and virginal Ophelia, abandoned by reason and her lover—that prince from a kingdom where everything was rotten. Yes, water was the ultimate refuge for women who were too beautiful and too proud for a world devoted to every kind of rottenness and insanity—including their own. And she, for whom the world was more dirty and chaotic, she, for whom the insanity was more terrible, had to follow their path. She, who so resembled them, even though she was far from matching their renown—hers was a misleading sort of first name—she could share their fate.* She, who had grown up so close to the sea but who had never had the right to contemplate it, to swim in it or to bare her legs, offering them to the water's soothing caress, would now give herself over to this blonder, calmer cousin, which seemed more welcoming in appearance but just as mysterious. She, who was born on a

* In Arabic, the first name *Chahira* means "famous" or "renowned." —*Trans.*

wave that was prisoner to the clinging seaweed of obscurantism and had sought refuge in the Col de la Liberté, a name and reputation that was—just like her first name—nothing but a sweet lie, was at last going to find truth and light in the river's tenebrous soul.*

Tomorrow. Tomorrow was so close! And it would be a deliverance. No more rottenness. No more torture. No more pain. No more humiliation. Of course, her heavy, forty-year-old body—though a forties that defied the diktat of passing time—would not float with the young and frail Ophelia's grace. There would not be any water lilies surrounding her brown hair; the birds would not sing her an elegy. Her eyes, lamentably chestnut brown, would not fade into the azure water and horizon as certainly had the blue-green pair of the woman who sang *Layali el uns.* But the water would be gentle with her. Yes, she was sure of it. The water, so indifferent beneath the July sun, would open its arms with kindness. The water would take her lightly by the hand to accompany her to a better world.

---

* *Col de La Liberté,* the place name for a mountain pass near Chahira's hometown of El Moudja, signifies "Liberty Peak." As noted earlier, this is also the meaning of Tizi N'Tlelli.—*Trans.*

XXXIII

The Danube's blue water was still asleep beneath the embrace of the dawning sun and the nearby trees. Humans, masters in the art of disturbing any sort of quiet, had not yet disrupted the river god's rest; they, too, slept, earning their slumber after a long war against ghosts borne of a difficult day full of exhaustion, races against deadlines, aggravations and compromises made against principles and dignity. A war that, when not won through the intervention of that ultimate weapon, the sleeping pill, often rages on until morning, a war rife with stubborn nightmares and frequent abrupt and worried awakenings. No, the poor human creatures—mostly modern creatures—do not have the same good night's sleep as the one who keeps watch over the four European capitals.

It must have been 7:20 in the morning. Not fully awake, Chahira walked toward the endless stretch of water. Her sleep had been quite peaceful. For the first time in years she did not have to fight the satyrs' vicious stares or their obscene and sometimes violent acts. For the first time, the *merqouchettes'* laughter was gone, leaving room only for silence in the elegant and cold hotel room. Elegant, just as she would be for her farewell rendezvous with life; cold, just like the river water surely would be and just like her body, which would find refuge there for eternity.

She wore blue jeans, azure blue like the smiling sky, a short white tunic that matched her lace-up shoes, and a kind of gray cardigan she packed in her luggage, worried about the European climate people had said was chilly even in the middle of summer. She was happy with her outfit; she had paid attention to each detail: lovely pieces in pastels—she had to leave the scene with grace and joy—but also in fabrics heavy enough to accelerate her trip to the home that she had chosen in the depths. She looked around: she would surely find a few tidy, heavy stones to put in her cardigan's large pockets. The brilliant Virginia had a disciple.

"Hey, Chahira!"

She looked around for the source of the familiar voice that called her name and saw a tall brown-headed figure running toward her out of breath. What was he doing here this early in the morning? She thought it was early enough that she would not have to worry about chancing upon someone. Now what was there to be done? Hurry and let herself be swallowed up by the water that was so calm, yet so voracious? This was not how she imagined this final scene. She did not want to run. She wanted to move at a calm and proud pace and lie down in the water with the juvenile radiance of Ophelia or Asmahan's darker one. She wanted the sad yet majestic end of tragic heroines, not a burlesque scene of panic, gesticulation, and shouting.

But it was already too late. Ali—he was the one calling her name—had already caught up with her.

"*Wech bik,* you're acting like we don't know each other," he said with his typical good humor. "I ran out of breath trying to catch up with you, and you're acting like I don't exist!"*

He stopped for a moment to look at her, a glimmer of admiration evident in his eyes. Chahira, suddenly wide awake, could not help but laugh.

"I have to say, you're right to ignore me like that," he continued slowly, not taking his eyes off her. "You look like a true queen. These colors! And your eyes!"

"What are you doing here so early in the morning," she finally asked him, her voice calm but betraying a certain irritation.

"Oh, you were waiting for your prince!" he said with a wink. "Sorry for the intrusion."

She grew increasingly impatient.

"I have no prince and don't hope to find one. I wanted to be alone. Absolutely alone."

Her tone was dry, and she saw the young man's laughing face grew serious. Usually so jovial, so sure of himself, he was plainly offended. She felt all the serenity she had jealously protected

* "Wech bik" signifies: "What's the matter?"—*Trans.*

since the day before splinter apart. The voices, absent for several hours, returned to reproach her for the way she treated this kind friend. A kind friend, really? Or the devil in human form?

A hand pinched the tip of her breast in punishment. Mohand awoke grumbling and in a bad mood. Inhaling nervously, she suppressed a smell of smoked fish and smiled at Ali.

"I was running because I wanted to invite you to come with me to Bratislava. Did you know it's just seventy kilometers from here? I'd intended on going with Gerda, but she has plans to go to London for a huge contract . . ."

She stood in embarrassed silence.

"Of course, we can go pick up Warda," he added, thinking this was the reason for her reluctance.

"Well," she finally answered. "I have other plans . . ."

He looked at her, astonished. How could she have other plans? This girl knew nobody in Vienna; was this not the first time she had stepped foot in Europe? And what was she doing so early in the morning, alone by the Danube? He suddenly noticed that her face had traded its superb serenity for pallor and an unsettled gaze. He stepped closer and touched her arm. A distraught expression appeared on his face, as if he had a vague understanding of the young woman's plans.

"Are you sure everything is all right, Chahira?"

His voice, infinitely gentle, was just like the feel of his hand on her skin. She shivered with pleasure and fear at the same time. Who was this Ali? The young, airy, and grinning man who spoke so kindly to her, or the sadist who haunted her nightmares?

"Yes," she said, smiling again. "It's just that I'd wanted to enjoy a quiet moment in this magnificent place that I'll be leaving tomorrow."

"So," he replied with hesitation, "Bratislava doesn't interest you?"

She was silent. She did not know why a sudden desire to accept the invitation filled her.

"Go!" Nacer yelled, irritated.

"Go!" replied the *merqouchettes* in unison.

Mohand became sullen. He did not want her to leave with such a tall, cultivated, and self-assured, dark-haired man. The others fell silent, respecting his unhappiness.

"You don't want me to go, Mohand?" she said tenderly. The smell of fish again filled the air without her having time to stop it. Ali rubbed his nose, a slight grimace on his face. She suddenly remembered all of yesterday's humiliations. The smells, indiscreet sounds, the audience's laughter. No. She did not want to be ridiculed again, and least of all in front of this handsome man.

"Sorry, Ali," she grudgingly responded. "I want to spend this last day in Vienna. Have fun in Bratislava!"

The young man gave a disappointed smile. She watched him walk off with a painful stab in her heart.

Now what was she supposed to do? Walk toward the Danube's embrace, as she had planned? But nothing was as she had planned: neither the setting nor the main character. Torn from its sleep by solitary dreamers and a few couples looking for privacy, the Danube had already given up its role as calm and mysterious god, and she ceased to be the imperious heroine serenely confronting her fate; she turned back into the tormented woman she had always been, consumed by unspeakable fears and doubts. Why bother going out like that? Like a tired, frightened, and pathetic creature?

Now what was she supposed to do, she asked herself again. She had refused the Danube's call. She had refused Ali's invitation, which she had very much wanted to accept. When would she stop rejecting all invitations to life? And all invitations to death? She let herself collapse onto the wet grass, not worrying what would become of her brand-new cardigan and pants, and burst into tears.

"Don't cry," said Nacer, as he gently brushed her arm.

"Don't cry," the *merqouchettes* said in an emotional voice.

"Don't cry, Chahira," Mohand said at last, in a timid and embarrassed voice.

"You again, Mohand?" she heard herself say out loud.

A few passersby looked at her and walked quickly away, startled.

"I want nothing more to do with you, Mohand," she continued in her head. "I want nothing more to do with any of you! Why are you pretending to be nice now when you have poisoned my life for years? Leave! Get out of my space!"

The shadows, stricken by her reproach, kept quiet. Mohand went off to sit a few meters away, muttering apologies.

What was she supposed to do now? The only thing she could do was reunite with the ghosts who controlled her life and thoughts. This moment she was spending with them now, hearing their warm words and their sincere support, was nice. After all, those who made decisions about the lives of others did not have as much compassion or heart.

Tomorrow, the plane would take her back to that country where the fate of forty million men and women was held hostage by decision makers much more tyrannical and far less human than her own. Compatriots would still try to flee their yokes and, like her, find themselves devoured by water, the traitorous water of the Mediterranean. And yet, these compatriots, whom she had always judged harshly and about whom she had stubbornly refused to see anything but faults, proved to have more courage than she did. They did not allow themselves to be beaten down; they forced themselves to have plans, to make themselves beautiful, to keep smiling, to celebrate, to laugh, and to sing. And maybe one day in El Moudja, in Tizi N'Tlelli, and everywhere else in that country doomed to disorder, fears, and humiliations just as her own mind was, maybe one day in those places laughter and song would ring out, free and sonorous, defying all tyranny, all hypocrisy, and all ugliness.

"Mohand, sing me one of your songs," she suddenly said.

The ghost-singer moved more awkwardly and lumbering than ever and sat down next to her.

"I will sing you whatever song you like, but no more talk of tragic heroines' stories or of embracing the Danube."

"If you promise to always be by my side," she said with a wink.

"Always," he said, shyly patting her shoulder.

The other shadows clapped. She gently placed her head on the artist's shoulder, smiling. A feeling of infinite well-being took hold of her.

"I promise, Mohand," she said with a resolute voice. "And so, how about that song?"

AFTERWORD

Mildred Mortimer

The Emergence of Algerian Literature in French

As a new generation of writers emerges in Algerian fiction, bringing new concerns, perspectives, and aesthetic innovations to literature, it is pertinent to contextualize their writings within the historical and linguistic framework in which they originated. Beginning in the early 1950s, a francophone literature emerged in North Africa written by *colonisés,* indigenous Arab and Berber colonial subjects who had attended French colonial schools and mastered the language of the colonizer. Expressing the profound alienation of a colonized population, the "generation of 1952," as it came to be known, included Algerian writers Mouloud Feraoun, Mohammed Dib, Kateb Yacine, and Assia Djebar, all of whom became major figures in the realm of francophone literature, with their work appearing over the years in English translation in the CARAF series.

Exposing the injustices of colonialism—the appropriation of indigenous land by the settlers, separate legal and educational systems for the colonized, French citizenship denied to Algerian Muslims—all of which resulted in few possibilities for social and economic advancement for the colonized, these writers also sought to represent their own lives authentically to both Europeans and their own communities, aware, however, that most colonial subjects were illiterate. Mouloud Feraoun's *Le fils du pauvre* (*The Poor Man's Son* [1950]) depicted the poverty of rural Kabylia. Mohammed Dib's *La grande maison* (The big house [1952]) shed light on urban poverty in the western part of the country. Kateb Yacine's *Nedjma* [1956] turned to poetic realism to explore myth, history, and the Algerian collective unconscious. Assia Djebar's *Les enfants du nouveau monde* (*Children of the New World* [1962]) added a new dimension to the corpus by depicting women's roles in the anticolonial struggle, revealing their growing political awareness and self-affirmation by assuming new responsibilities during the war.

A theme that emerges in Algerian writing from the early texts to the present day is the difficult relationship that Algeria has had with France since the colonial era. Historically, all three nations of the Maghreb—Algeria, Morocco, and Tunisia—experienced colonial conquest, yet only Algeria, defeated by France in 1830, became an integral part of France; as protectorates, Tunisia and Morocco retained their political identity. Moreover, France, in 1956, granted independence to Tunisia and Morocco while fighting a war to keep Algeria French.

Historians confirm that Algerian independence was won through a long and violent process. By the time the eight-year bitter conflict ended in 1962, possibly a million Algerian lives had been lost; more than three million rural Algerians had been displaced from their homes; and hundreds of villages had been razed, and fields, pastures and forests destroyed. In addition, most *pieds-noirs* (French Algerians) fled the country, some fearing reprisal at the hands of Algerians, others convinced that there was no place for them in the new nation. Many *harkis* (Algerians who had collaborated with the French colonials) were killed in retribution by Algerians, with others relocated to camps in France. The newly independent nation was faced with millions of impoverished, uprooted peasants, a population poorly equipped for the next phase of Algerian history (Ruedy, 190).

Understandably, at independence and in the decades that followed, a multitude of political, economic, social, cultural, and linguistic issues would arise, and in this postcolonial period, Algerian writers soon became critics of the new order. For example, Rachid Mimouni's novel *Le fleuve détourné* (The diverted river [1982]) centers upon the plight of an Algerian villager who returns home at independence only to confront postwar corruption, the betrayal of revolutionary ideals, and the abuse of power in the newly independent nation. Mouloud Mammeri's *La traversée* (The desert crossing), published the same year, uses allegory, a journalist's crossing of the Sahara, to express the same sense of disillusionment in postcolonial

Algeria. During this period of the 1980s, Assia Djebar published *L'amour, la fantasia* (*Fantasia: An Algerian Cavalcade* [1985]), a distinctly feminist novel that combines autobiographical fragments with colonial history and oral narratives of women who had participated actively in the Algerian War of Independence to show the legacy of French colonialism and indigenous patriarchy combining to contribute to the silencing Algerian women.

Thus, we find that Algerian writers who had previously exposed the injustices of the colonial order turn their attention to postcolonial issues, with many, if not most, choosing to write in French and not in Arabic, which, at independence, had become the nation's official language. After a long political struggle, Tamazight (often referred to as Kabyle, since the Berber language is spoken mainly in the Kabyle region of Algeria) obtained the same official status in 2016. Yet, by adopting the French language to evoke the changing realities of their inner and outer worlds, Algerian writers of Arab and Berber origin are nevertheless aware of the ambiguity of writing in the former colonizer's language.

Recognizing the link between language and colonization, Tunisian writer Albert Memmi, in his *Anthologie des écrivains maghrébins d'expression française,* a collection that appeared in 1965, three years after the end of Algeria's anticolonial war, expressed the concern that francophone literature of the Maghreb was marked for extinction. French, the language of the colonizer, he concluded, was a vestige of the French colonial presence in North Africa, a legacy of past oppression that would have no place in the new postcolonial era. Memmi believed that once Arabic replaced French as the language of instruction throughout the three countries of the Maghreb, francophone writers would lose their reading public. Hence, the writers whose work figure in his anthology would come to represent a moment in history. Predicting a paucity of francophone Maghrebi readers, he wrote: "Isn't it paradoxical, indeed disquieting for the future of his work that the writer, because he uses French, cannot be understood at home?" (19).

Memmi was joined in this view by Algerian poet and novelist Malek Haddad, who saw himself as an *orphelin de lecteurs* (9)—a writer without the public he wished to reach—and chose to fall silent at independence in 1962. Both writers recognized that as francophone writers of the Maghreb, they were members of an elite educated in French colonial schools in contrast to the indigenous populations, Arabic- and Berber-speaking men and women who were largely illiterate. In addition, they viewed literature as an expression of alienation, revolt, and contestation tied to a specific historical period that had just come to an end. Far too pessimistic concerning the role that francophone literature would play in the postcolonial era, Memmi and Haddad could not envisage the Algerian writer's critical role in independent Algeria nor the bumpy road that lay ahead as the new nation emerged from under the yoke of colonialism. Neither writer could predict the dark decade of the 1990s, the era of Algeria's civil war between the Algerian government and Islamic fundamentalism that would eventually claim more than 120,000 lives and send many secular French-educated individuals into exile.

During this tumultuous period, as secular men and women became the targets of Islamic extremists, and women who refused to wear the veil in public risked their lives, Algerian women's voices grew increasingly stronger. The "nouvelles femmes d'Alger" (new women of Algiers), as Djebar calls them (*Oran, langue morte*, 367), writers such as Malika Mokkedem and Maïssa Bey (both of whose texts appear in the CARAF series) joined Djebar in creating a women's literature of resistance.[1] Vehemently criticizing Islamic fundamentalists for religious intolerance, they blamed the government for corruption and for failing to promote a democracy that would guarantee equal rights for all its citizens. Protesting the Family Code of 1984, which relegates women to second-class citizens, they challenged Algeria's patriarchal culture which impedes women's emotional growth and professional advancement. In the new millennium, the corpus of Algerian women's literature has grown to include the testimonial literature of women who had actively participated in Algeria's War of Independence. Former combatants such as Zohra Drif and Louisette Ighilahriz, writing their memoirs in their later years, offer readers personal reflections upon a life shaped by political engagement. Thus, despite Memmi's concern that francophone literature of Algeria and her neighbors would quickly disappear, it has continued to thrive in the six decades that have passed since the end of French colonialism in the Maghreb. Existing in a linguistic context in which Arabic and Tamazight are official languages, and French is not, it nevertheless remains a literature of contestation, revolt, interrogation, and aesthetic innovation.

A New Voice in Algerian Fiction

Poet, novelist, short story writer, essayist, and literature critic, Lynda Chouiten is an important new voice in Algerian fiction. Born in Tizi-Ouzou, Algeria, in 1977, she belongs to a generation of Algerian writers born after the anticolonial struggle. While some of her contemporaries write in French, others in Arabic, and still others in Tamazight, she chooses to write in French, although integrating brief passages of Arabic and Tamazight into her texts. She explains:

French is the language with which I'm most at ease. I often repeat that French is not a foreign language for me; I've been familiar with it ever since I was a child—even before I went to school. My parents, who are both educated, have always spoken a mixture of Kabyle and French, and it is this mixture that I call my mother language. But because I've never learned Kabyle at school—never learned to read and write it—it was inevitable that French would soon be the language I master best.

You see, I've grown up in a francophone environment, which determined my linguistic orientation; so, although I did read in Arabic, I read at least twice as much in French. In turn, this made French come to me more naturally than any other language. I know its grammar, its vocabulary, its subtleties, but more importantly, I express both my complex thoughts and my deepest feelings in it. It is commonly admitted that one's strongest and unaffected feelings spontaneously express themselves in one's mother tongue; mine come out in a mixture of French and Kabyle, the two languages on which my parents and the books I've read fed me.

Later, other languages added themselves to the list: standard Arabic, Arabic dialects, English, and small bits of other languages. This linguistic (and cultural) hybridity defines me and characterizes my writings, which, although written in French, also comprise words and idiomatic expressions borrowed from different languages. In a sense, therefore, my texts are written less in French than in a linguistic mix in which French dominates.[2]

Professor of English at the University of Boumerdès in Algeria, Chouiten is both a literary scholar and a fiction writer. She completed a doctorate in literature at the National University of Ireland, Galway, writing her dissertation on the life and writings of Isabelle Eberhardt, the early twentieth-century francophone writer of Russian background and Swiss nationality whose fiction, journals, and letters reflect her extensive travels through the Algerian Sahara.[3] Fluent in Arabic and a convert to Islam, Eberhardt frequently dressed as a man and smoked *kif* publicly, gaining notoriety for her flamboyant and iconoclastic lifestyle. The tragic nature of her death at the age of twenty-seven in a flash flood in the Sahara reinforced the romantic image of the young writer whose life ended too soon, her literary corpus including manuscripts retrieved from the flood waters that took her life. In her study of Eberhardt's life and work, Chouiten examines the writer's relationship to both the indigenous populations of the Sahara and the French colonial agents, for whom she may very well have engaged in espionage. Challenging the representation of Eberhardt as a rebellious and iconoclastic figure, she emphasizes the writer's conservatism, her embrace of European colonial, racist, and patriarchal attitudes of her times.

The year 2019 was an exceptional one in the novelist's literary career. A finalist the previous year for two literary prizes, the Prix Mohammed Dib and L'Escale d'Alger, for her first novel, *Le roman des pov' cheveux*, she won the Prix Assia Djebar in 2019 for her second, *Une valse*, securing her place in contemporary Algerian fiction. Although both texts offer the reader a sociopolitical critique of Algerian society, they are distinctly different in terms of tone. Humor enlivens the first, an allegorical satire in which strands of hair describe and deride human foibles. A sense of darkness and foreboding permeates the second, a distinctly feminist text that probes the relationship between woman's creativity and madness in a patriarchal world in which women's dreams are far too often shattered. Since the publication of these two novels, she has published a collection of short stories, *Des rêves à leur portée* (Dreams within their reach [2022]); a collection of poetry, *J'ai connu les deserts et autres poèmes* (I have known deserts and other poems [2023]); and a fairy tale, *Les pierres du pays des Baggans* (The stones of the land of the Baggans [2023].

In *A Waltz,* the writer asks how a woman with a creative mind, artistic talent, and rebellious spirit can make her way in a patriarchal, conservative, and confining society. To place this question within a contemporary Algerian context, she charts the journey of a dressmaker from a small town in Algeria to an international fashion design competition in Vienna. This journey would represent a significant step toward empowerment were it not for the inner demons that accompany the protagonist every step of the way. The demands of daily life anchor Chahira Lahab to the real world, but the demons, hallucinations, and fears that haunt her imagination constantly threaten her grip on reality. Thus, as she fights against the constraints of patriarchy, she battles mental illness. Chouiten has explained in a public discussion of her novel that by introducing the theme of madness as a response to societal constraints, her text conforms to the analysis elaborated by feminist critics Susan Gilbert and Sandra Gubar in *The Madwoman in the Attic* (1979), a study of Victorian women's writing. The title of their work refers to Charlotte Brontë's *Jane Eyre,* a classic nineteenth-century British novel in which mad Bertha is locked in her husband's attic. Exploring the relationship between societal constraints and madness in Victorian fiction, the critics find female protagonists responding with madness to their silencing, oppression, and imprisonment by the patriarchal order.

As Gilbert and Gubar argue that anglophone women writers confined to restricted spaces by society developed strategies of escape—among them madness—through fiction, critic Valérie Orlando, in her study, *Of Suffocated Hearts and Tortured*

Souls, (2003), extends their analysis to francophone literature of Africa and the Caribbean. Referencing anglophone women writers of the nineteenth and twentieth centuries—a list that includes the Brontë sisters, Emily Dickinson, and Virginia Woolf—Orlando explains that francophone postcolonial authors use their heroines' madness as a catalyst to explore their protagonists' psyche, as well as the sociocultural, political, and historical factors that influence them, and the author's environment as well (66).

Examining Algerian fiction, we can find numerous examples of the mad female character, the woman who has lost her grip on reality, beginning in the 1950s. For example, in Feraoun's *Le fils du pauvre* (*The Poor Man's Son* [1950]), the protagonist's aunt loses her mind following the unexpected death of her sister. In Yamina Mechakra's *La grotte éclatée* (The shattered cave [1979]), the nurse caring for wounded and dying Algerian combatants experiences mental confusion following the bombing of her underground hospital. In Nina Bouraoui's *La voyeuse interdite* (*Forbidden Vision* [1991]), a young Algerian woman sequestered at puberty by her Islamic fundamentalist father, slips into madness. If in the first novel, madness is due to personal trauma, and in the second, to the trauma of war, the third presents mental confusion as a response to patriarchal oppression. Bouraoui's Fikria and Chouiten's Chahira also turn to madness as an escape from reality when their dreams are shattered, their ambitions thwarted.

A Waltz: A Quest Narrative

Structuring her novel as a quest narrative, one in which the protagonist journeys forth, facing a series of tests on the path to maturity, Chouiten situates the text in three geographical spaces: El Moudja, a fictional coastal town in the Kabyle region of Algeria; Tizi N'Tlelli, a pseudonym for Tizi-Ouzou, the regional capital of Kabylia; and Vienna, the capital of Austria. Each location denotes a section of the work and marks a step forward in the quester's journey.[4]

The first, El Moudja, is the small, primarily Arabic-speaking town where Chahira was raised and now has her dressmaking business. Significantly, the very name of her town disappoints her. As she explains, the town of El Moudja, "the wave" in Arabic, has neither physical charm nor a beautiful seafront. Indeed, for the forty-year-old woman who, despite family pressure, has chosen not to marry, it signifies a confining space from which she longs to escape. Most significantly, it is the place where, in adolescence, her dream of broadening her world through education is shattered. As Chahira prepares to finish secondary school with honors, her father discovers an erotic poem that she had written and promptly withdraws her from school. This traumatic event occurs during the dark decade of the 1990s, when Islamic fundamentalists were publicly harassing Algerian women who refuse to wear the veil. To avoid any aggression she might encounter in the streets of her town as an unveiled woman, she apprentices herself to a dressmaker in her apartment building. Thus, the adolescent who once moved freely in public space now finds herself confined, and although dressmaking proves to be an appropriate outlet for her creative temperament, it does not assuage her sense of loss and despair. As she notes: "Hell was also this: seeing herself forbidden to reach the end of her studies, just a few months before the end of her secondary education, when she was so bright" (10).

With familial and societal pressures increasing over the years, Chahira, in her early thirties, shows signs of mental illness: disturbing nightmares in which phantom predators molest her; panic attacks in which she imagines fluids and odors emanating uncontrollably from her body; and imaginary encounters with fictitious foes—the *merqouchettes*, harpies who mock and harass her, as well as two imaginary companions, Mohand, the musician, and Nacer, the intellectual, who offer her their support.

Following a dispute with her family, which does not support her as she struggles with her illness, she decides to leave El Moudja for Tizi N'Tlelli in the hope that the regional capital will grant her the freedom she seeks, the opportunities unavailable in her small hometown, and respite from the chaos in her mind. By leaving home, she rejects the house of patriarchy, turning her back on an oppressive family, while affirming her independence and embracing her illness: "Now her pride was in revolt, and she blessed her illness—it filled her with a new-found power and stifled her fear. [. . .] She knew that what was called madness was nothing other than the lofty call of freedom celebrating the 'I's' triumph and giving a full-throated laugh at the pitiable conventions that it superbly destroyed" (49). Thus, Chahira, like the Victorian heroine, adopts madness as a liberating strategy in her struggle against patriarchal and societal conventions and constraints.

Yet, Tizi N'Tlelli, "Liberty Peak" in Tamazight, proves to be a misnomer. If the city once promised liberty, the thwarted Berber Spring of the 1980s,[5] the dark decade of the 1990s, and residual patriarchal attitudes quickly dashed any hopes of greater possibilities for a woman, particularly a single woman seeking a more open society. When Chahira attempts to rent an apartment in Tizi N'Tlelli, a series of prospective landlords, suspicious of the motives of an unmarried woman, turn her down. Moreover, the city comes to signify personal tragedy for her when young thugs vandalize the shop that had supplied her with lace and fine fabric, killing its elderly proprietor, her closest friend. So much for the dream of a better life in Tizi N'Tlelli, and so much for the dream of leaving her hallucinations behind; they grow stronger, the boundaries between the real and the imaginary increasingly blurred.

Leaving Tizi N'Tlelli for Vienna when her entry is chosen for an international fashion competition, Chahira hopes to fulfill her dream of gaining recognition in the world of fashion, and the purely romantic notion of dancing to a Viennese waltz with a dashing partner. This city first sparked her imagination when she heard Asmahan, the legendary Syrian singer, sing of its magical charm in Arabic: *Layali el uns fi Vienna*—oh nights spent in Vienna! While in Vienna, she visits the Hofburg Palace and is drawn to a portrait of Empress Elisabeth, wife of Emperor Franz Joseph I, which she discovers on the palace walls. As she studies the portrait, she begins to view the legendary queen, known to the world as Sisi, as her kindred spirit, a woman who physically resembles her—the same complexion, long auburn hair, and faraway look—and who shares her love of the arts, particularly poetry. Yet, Ali, a fellow fashion designer and compatriot, warns her that the queen's life story, although admittedly extraordinary—her marriage to Emperor Franz Joseph I, the death of her son in a murder-suicide pact at Meyerling, and her own death at the hands of an anarchist—has been overly romanticized both in literature and in film. Most importantly, he notes that Sisi played the role assigned to her in life, but Chahira has gone beyond her prescribed role to forge her own destiny: "You make your own designs; you're the ambassador for what is beautiful in your country . . . And if you are here in Vienna, it's due to your own merit!" (116).

Yet, despite her success in the Austrian capital—she places well at the competition and dances with a handsome young Austrian at the ball—Chahira's hallucinations intensify, and with them, her despair. As dark thoughts engage her mind, she finds herself drawn to the Danube, tempted to follow in the footsteps of British novelist Virginia Woolf, who, she recalls, weighted her pockets with stones, walked into a river near her home in England, and drowned. Chahira does indeed approach the banks of the Danube, but pauses, and turns away. Although the twentieth-century writer draws her to the brink, her inner strength keeps her from self-destruction. With the clarity of vision that until now has eluded her comes the realization that she must control her fears, defeat her demons, and find the inner calm with which to face the future. With her friend and colleague Ali offering her a position in Algiers, it is possible that upon her return to Algeria, she will leave the regional capital of Kabylia for the nation's capital, Algiers, thereby widening her horizons as she continues her journey to self-understanding and empowerment.

A well-constructed and well-written novel, Chouiten's text is original in several aspects. First, by depicting a protagonist who, when unable to continue her studies, excels in the realm of artistic design, the novelist pays tribute to Algerian women who express their creativity through artisanal works—weaving, embroidery, and pottery—all of which engage women's skills in ways different from those of writers, but equally expressive. Second, by situating the fashion competition in Vienna rather than in Paris, the center of haute couture and the capital of the former colonial power, she introduces a historic European city rarely depicted in Algerian literature. Choosing Vienna, the former capital of the Austro-Hungarian Empire, with its impressive vestiges of empire apparent in the city's architecture, art, and music, the novelist not only adds an international dimension to the text but also eschews the more common paradigm of France/Algeria that conveys the fraught relationship between the former colonizer and colonized that has marked Algerian fiction since its beginnings.

As the "generation of 1952" expressed their alienation as *colonisés* in which they constantly faced constraints, Chouiten's Chahira wrestles with the rise of Islamic fundamentalism and the vestiges of indigenous patriarchy in Algeria, both of which limit women's possibilities. Significantly, until Chahira leaves her homeland for a brief but transformative stay in Vienna, she lives in the Berber region of Kabylia. Thus, as the writer charts the journey of a dynamic young woman with a creative mind, artistic bent, and rebellious spirit making her way in a patriarchal, conservative, and confining society, she situates her protagonist in the same geographic region of Algeria that she calls home. Defining her relationship to Kabyle culture, she writes:

> I don't necessarily write with my Kabyleness in mind and I don't like being systematically brought back to my Kabyle identity. Although my novels are (at least partly) set in Kabylia, I try to write texts that explore human issues and complexity in a way that transcends frontiers and with which any reader, regardless of their nationality or culture, can relate. Having said that, Kabylia is strongly present in *A Waltz*, which is partly set in Tizi N'Tlelli, meaning Liberty Peak. Choosing this name for this city which is nothing but the fictionalized version of Tizi-Ouzou, my hometown, is both symbolical and ironic. More than any other Algerian region, Kabylia is known to have been an "enlightened" place that is not too tough on women, that has always rejected religious extremism and fought for political rights, the long-confiscated identity, and individual liberties; however, this reputation of openness is mocked in my novel, as Chahira, the protagonist, faces misogyny and bigotry in this very Tizi N'Tlelli that she used to idealize

as a place of freedom. With disappointment, she discovers a city that teems with bearded men and veiled women, landlords that refuse to rent her a house because she is a single woman, and conversations that equate women's emancipation with brazenness. Through the character of Chahira, I offer a critical, albeit fond eye on this region of mine—Kabylia—underscoring its contradictions and its oscillation between an aspiration to freedom and equality, on the one hand, and its inability to turn its back on worn-out traditions, the weight of religion, and sexist reflexes, on the other hand.[6]

Published in 2019, the year that saw Algeria's Hirak, the massive demonstrations throughout the country that led to the fall of former president Abdelaziz Bouteflika, *A Waltz* clearly captures the mood of the times. Algerians whose dreams of wider horizons and a freer society had been shattered opted for change, cautiously optimistic as they took to the streets, envisioning an uncertain future. Similarly, in the realm of fiction, Chahira Lahab, her journey to self-understanding and empowerment drawing to completion, returns to Algeria and, like her compatriots, faces her uncertain future with guarded optimism.

Notes

1. For a study of Algerian women's resistance literature of the dark decade of the 1990s, see Ireland.
2. Email correspondence from Lynda Chouiten to Mildred Mortimer, January 14, 2024.
3. Published as *Isabelle Eberhardt and North Africa: A Carnivalesque Mirage* (2015).
4. An earlier version of the analysis that follows appeared as a book review in the *Journal of North African Studies* 27, no. 4 (2022): 847–50.
5. The Berber Spring was a period of political protest in 1980, claiming recognition of the Berber identity and language in Algeria. See Aïtel.
6. Email correspondence from Lynda Chouiten to Mildred Mortimer, January 14, 2024.

BIBLIOGRAPHY

Aïtel, Fazia. *We Are Imazighen: The Development of Algerian Berber Identity in Twentieth-Century Literature and Culture.* Gainesville: University Press of Florida, 2014.

Bey, Maïssa. *Entendez-vous dans les Montagnes.* . . . La Tour d'Aigues: Éditions de l'Aube, 2002. Translated by Erin Lamm as *Do You Hear in the Mountains . . . and Other Stories,* CARAF Books (Charlottesville: University of Virginia Press, 2018).

———. *Nouvelles d'Alger.* Paris: Grasset, 1998.

Bouraoui, Nina. *La voyeuse interdite.* Paris: Gallimard, 1991. Translated by K. Melissa Marcus as *Forbidden Vision* (Barrytown, N.Y.: Station Hill, 1995).

Chouiten, Lynda. *Des rêves à leur portée.* Algiers: Casbah Éditions, 2022.

———. *Isabelle Eberhardt and North Africa: A Carnivalesque Mirage.* Lanham, Md.: Lexington Books, 2015.

———. *J'ai connu les déserts: Et autres poèmes.* Brive-la-Gaillarde: Éditions Constellations, 2023.

———. *Le roman des pôv cheveux.* Algiers: Casbah Éditions, 2017.

———. *Les pierres du pays des Baggans.* Tizi-Ouzou: Talsa, 2023.

———. *Une valse.* Algiers: Casbah Éditions, 2019.

Dib, Mohammed. *La grande maison.* Paris: Seuil, 1952.

Djebar, Assia. *L'amour, la fantasia.* Paris: Jean Lattès, 1985; Paris: Albin Michel, 1995. Translated by Dorothy S. Blair as *Fantasia, An Algerian Cavalcade* (London: Quartet Books, 1985).

———. *Les enfants du nouveau monde.* Paris: Julliard, 1962. Translated by Marjolijn de Jager as *Children of the New World: A Novel of the Algerian War* (New York: Feminist Press, 2005).

———. *Oran, langue morte.* Paris: Actes Sud, 1997.

Drif, Zohra. *Mémoires d'une combattante de l'ALN: Zone Autonome d'Alger.* Algiers: Chihab Éditions, 2013. Translated by Andrew Ferrand as *Inside the Battle of Algiers* (Charlottesville, Va.: Just World Books, 2017).

Feraoun, Mouloud. *Le fils du pauvre: Menrad, instituteur Kabyle.* Le Puy, France: Le Cahiers du Nouvel Humanisme, 1950; repr. Seuil, 1954. Translated by Lucy R. McNair as *The Poor Man's Son: Menrad, Kabyle Schoolteacher,* CARAF Books (Charlottesville: University of Virginia Press, 2005).

Gilbert, Sandra M., and Susan Gubar. *The Madwoman in the Attic.* New Haven, Conn.: Yale University Press, 1979.

Haddad, Malek. *Le malheur en danger.* Paris: La Nef de Paris, 1956.

Ighilahriz, Louisette. *Algérienne,* récit recueilli par Anne Nivat. Paris: Fayard/Calmann-Lévy, 2001.

Ireland, Susan. "Voices of Resistance in Contemporary Algerian Women's Writing." In *Maghrebian Mosaic: A Literature in Transition,* edited by Mildred Mortimer. Boulder: Lynne Rienner, 2001. 171–93.

Kateb, Yacine. *Nedjma.* Paris: Seuil, 1956. Translated by Richard Howard as *Nedjma,* CARAF Books (Charlottesville: University of Virginia Press, 1991).

Mammeri, Mouloud. *La traversée.* Paris: Plon, 1982.

Mechakra, Yamina. *La grotte éclatée.* Algiers: Editions S.N.E.D., 1979.

Memmi, Albert. *Anthologie des écrivains maghrébins d'expression française.* Paris: Présence Africaine, 1965.

Mimouni, Rachid. *Le fleuve détourné.* Paris: Robert Laffont, 1982.

Mokeddem, Malika. *Des rêves et des assassins.* Paris: Grasset, 1995. Translated by K. Melissa Marcus as *Of Dreams and Assassins,* CARAF Books (Charlottesville: University of Virginia Press, 2000).

———. *L'interdite.* Paris: Grasset, 1993.

Orlando, Valérie. *Of Suffocated Hearts and Tortured Souls: Seeking Subjecthood through Madness in Francophone Women's Writing of Africa and the Caribbean.* Lanham, Md.: Lexington Books, 2003.

Ruedy, John Douglas. *Modern Algeria: The Origins and Development of a Nation.* Bloomington: Indiana University Press, 1992; repr. 2005.